Memoir of a Doomsday Prophet

By

Randall DeVallance

For information, or to order additional copies, please contact:

Beacon Publishing Group
P.O. Box 41573 Charleston, S.C. 29423
800.817.8480| beaconpublishinggroup.com

Publisher's catalog available by request.

ISBN-13: 978-1-949472-31-8

ISBN-10: 1-949472-31-8

Published in 2021. New York, NY 10001.

First Edition. Printed in the USA.

Memoir of a Doomsday Prophet

Table of Contents

Chapter 1

My life had teetered on a precipice for so long that I hardly knew how to act now that everything had finally come crashing down. It's not true to say that I had no choice in the matter, that I was simply a victim of circumstance. Had I done one thing differently the entire story might have changed. Instead, I sat back and let it all happen.

There's a psychological phenomenon I read about once. A man standing at the foot of a hill sees a large boulder come loose at the peak and begin rolling down the hillside. End over end it tumbles, picking up speed. It seems to be heading more or less toward where the man is standing. The hill is tall, and there's still a long time before the boulder can roll all the way down, plenty of time for the man to move to a different spot where the boulder is less likely to land. He can't go backwards, away from the hill; not far behind him is a cliff, and a 300-foot drop to the sea below. But the path snaking around the foot of the hill is open to him and free of debris. He can move to his left or his right. He can walk, or he can run. Options exist.

Only the man doesn't move. First of all, he's not sure the boulder is actually rolling toward the spot where he's standing. The boulder is still so far up the hillside, you see, and its trajectory is hard to determine. It looks like it's headed toward him, but who knows? What if he takes off running and goes the wrong way? What if he inadvertently puts himself in the boulder's path, when he could have just stayed where he was and been safe? So he waits, trying to get a better read on which direction the boulder will choose. Sometimes it seems to be veering left, only to glance off an outcrop and turn back to the right, or vice versa. The man waits some more, thinking that once the boulder is past the rocky upperslope and reaches the grassy area further down its path will become clear. But even then, the terrain is uneven and the boulder still far enough away that he can't be certain it's actually heading toward him. He decides to play it safe and wait right where he is, observing and analyzing. The boulder keeps rolling, picking up speed.

Halfway down the slope. The man waits.

Three-quarters of the way down. The man waits.

At last the man can see how fast the boulder is moving, not rolling so much as bounding down the hillside, skipping tens of feet at a time. The dreadful realization sinks in that there's no longer time to move. The boulder is approaching so rapidly that even if the man immediately starts running as fast as he can in either direction it will be upon him before he can clear the area. The only thing he can do is wait where he is, make himself as small as possible and pray the boulder misses him.

The man crouches and tucks himself into a ball, like an armadillo taking refuge inside its shell. He says a prayer to a God he may or may not believe exists. It's an unpolished prayer, which is the best kind – an unqualified request for help, no empty promises or words of praise. God, if there is such a being, presumably has no time for artifice, being omniscient and all. "Give it to me straight" – I don't believe that line appears anywhere in a major religious text, but it should. It's a nice foundational principle for a religion. A God of Honesty. Truth as a deity. I think I'm on to something here. But then I've thought that before.

By the way, the man was crushed by the boulder.

That was the point of the story. Sometimes we're so afraid of taking the wrong action that we take no action at all. And that, in the end, is what kills us. Psychologists can vouch for this. They invented the anecdote after all, not me.

I did add the part about the prayer, though. Strunk and White would call that a "literary flourish".

Strunk and White wrote 'The Elements of Style', a handy little book about how to write a sentence, and then how best to put one sentence after another. Don't get fancy, is Strunk and White's advice. Don't beat around the bush. The cat killed the mouse. The mouse was not killed by the cat. This is advice our theoretical God can get behind.

Unless of course it's the mouse you care about, and you don't give one whit about the cat. There are exceptions to every rule. The man was crushed by the boulder. The boulder did not crush the man. They were not zealots, Strunk and White. They sympathized with the human condition.

I sympathize too. How can you not, once you know the truth? The 'Truth', I'm talking about now, the one and only God, in this universe anyway. And the truth is that everything that has happened and everything that will happen is happening right now. Not a new concept, but why would you think the truth would be something new? Quite the opposite – it has always been and always will be. There are no choices. Everything has already been written.

Which undercuts my earlier anecdote, now that I think about it. The man was always going to be crushed by the boulder. The boulder was always going to crush the man. He didn't run because he couldn't. He never ran, and so he never will run.

How do I know this? Aliens told me, in a dream.

I know how that sounds.

But I don't need to convince you. Theoretical physicists are already coming to the same conclusion. They call it the 'block-universe'. Psychologists will get there eventually. Then they can update their anecdotes. They probably already have, somewhere in the block-universe. Let's hope so. There's only so long you can go on telling the same old stories.

I mention that to them whenever they come to visit me. Twice a week, I think it is, or maybe three times. Time has a way of losing its meaning here, but then time has no meaning, as I've already told you.

Anyway, the psychologists come to my room every so often and sit and talk with me. There are four or five altogether, but two principals – Dr. Susan, a middle-aged woman with a blond bob who looks like someone's childless aunt, and my favorite, Dr. Steve, balding and bespectacled and speaking in an accent that has so far defied easy classification. Is it English, I wonder? Scandinavian? Transatlantic? I must remember to broach the subject someday, when Dr. Steve's not in one of his moods.

Mostly the doctors ask me questions, sometimes open-ended and sometimes pointed, but always probing. Whereas Dr. Susan's manner evinces a sort of pity for what she takes to be my broken condition, Dr. Steve can barely contain his condescension. "Is it your contention," he spluttered, eyes agog, to provide just one example, "based on this philosophy you've espoused, that you had no agency in your actions and are therefore completely free of blame?" I thrill at his scoffing tone, the inherent challenge behind it. How do I explain the truth to him in a way he'll understand? I am wholly innocent, yet guilty. The things I did I have always done, and will continue to do until the universe's end. I am like the man standing at the bottom of the hill, and the boulder is like BB, whom I'll tell you about in a moment.

That was a metaphor, though not a good one. If you're going to use a metaphor, make it count. That would be Strunk and White's advice.

I need to listen more.

Chapter 2

What I said before wasn't true.

That last passage was actually a simile, not a metaphor. A simile, according to Merriam-Webster, is a figure of speech comparing two unlike things using the word "like" or "as". A metaphor compares two things directly, eschewing "like" or "as".

BB was a boulder careening down the hill toward me. That's a metaphor.

Technically, Merriam-Webster classifies a simile as a *type* of metaphor. So I wasn't wrong before, so much as inexact. I like being exact, which is one of the reasons I like reading the dictionary so much.

There's plenty of time to read when you're stuck in prison.

No more metaphors. From here on out everything I tell you will be the plain and simple truth. "Make every word tell," said Strunk and White. Omit all that is unnecessary. Strunk Jr. even got rid of the comma in his last name. That's how committed he was.

Facts are what I'll focus on. Given what I know now I have no reason to obfuscate or insert more of my literary flourishes. The facts are incredible enough without exaggeration. It started in college, as so many things do. Why don't I just jump in? Preface is superfluous.

Make every word tell.

Don't beat around the bush.

Ok then…

Chapter 3

I sat on a bench outside Waverly Hall surveying my surroundings, silently cataloguing everything I saw with a dumb literalness, like a newly freed prisoner reorienting himself with the outside world – the pallid gray sky; the lawn, damp with early May dew; the breeze scuttling a few, stray leaves left over from the previous winter down the walk. Someday, I was sure, when reflecting on this moment, these details would be imbued with great significance, but at the time they were conspicuously mundane, like a montage some amateur director concocted to represent the passage of time. A group of students congregating near the building's main doors burst into laughter, bringing me back to the present. I looked down at my watch – just after nine. The thought was so preposterous I started grinning. It was obscene for momentous events to occur so early in the morning. What did one do with the rest of a day that had started like this one? How to fill the hours until sleep provided the necessary interlude to be able to put something like what had just happened into perspective?

Up until that point my life had been an object lesson in the power of taking success for granted. Whatever I lacked in ambition and seriousness I more than made up for in the cynical surety that I would continue to climb the ladder of achievement, rung after unearned rung, and find myself in the end more or less comfortable in the world. Life was a game, I had convinced myself, one that I had mastered. Though I possessed no great work ethic, I earned praise from my employers. Was no lover of people, yet charmed those in my company. Was no intellectual, yet breezed through my exams.

Until eventually, I didn't. Confidence gave way to arrogance. I began staying out late on weeknights, skipping classes, slipping into a life of debauchery as easily and naturally as a dowager queen into her late-husband's ermines. The few lectures I did bother to attend I tuned out the way young adults did in the days before smartphones, doodling in the margins of my notebook or – in those classrooms large enough to render me anonymous – listening to music on a Discman concealed within the lining of my jacket. My hangovers were often severe enough that no other distraction was necessary; I simply sat and meditated on the throbbing in my skull, like a medieval penitent holding his hand over a flame, until the professor declared the class to be over and released me from my suffering. The sum total of this behavior was that by my senior year I found myself in an unfamiliar position, failing multiple classes and on the verge of being placed on academic suspension.

Into this morass came a new problem. It was my great misfortune to encounter in that final year a professor worthy of the title, a man so engrossed in his subject matter that without it there was no lens through which he could meaningfully view the world. Beware the passionate ones, I always say. They can smell frauds like me a mile away. Nothing affronts a person like the Professor more than a cavalier attitude expressed toward his object of devotion – in this case, Classical Antiquity, with a focus on the late Roman Republic of the 2nd and 1st Centuries BCE.

Whatever you're thinking right now, despite what stray facts you may have picked up about Julius Caesar or Mark Antony or Cato or Cicero or any of the other names that continue ringing bells in our modern era, they would have been of no use in the classroom of Professor Hans Broadbent. Quite the opposite – he was just the sort of pedant who avoided incorporating common knowledge into his curriculum, and preferred students who came to his class as blank slates over those who regurgitated popular myths and trivia while considering themselves to be "somewhat educated" on the subject. Such shallow understanding worried Professor Broadbent to no end. "A little knowledge is a dangerous thing!" he was fond of exclaiming. It was common for the Professor to break off in the middle of some longwinded monologue about the shortsightedness of Sulla's eradication of his political enemies, hunch down over his desk, place his fingertips to his temples and lament, "Those who fail to learn from history are doomed to repeat it!" Trafficking in clichés, apparently, caused the Professor no such distress.

It was from Professor Broadbent's class that I had just come, for the second time that day. It was finals week at Braithwaite College, a small, colonial-era school in rural New England founded by Congregationalist ministers that was every bit as bucolic as that description suggests. The air hung heavy with a solemnity quite foreign to the place the rest of the semester. Students clustered together across the quad and in their dormitories and spoke with gravity about things like differentiable manifolds, the role of utilitarianism in modern markets, and ethnogenesis in the early Iron Age, the sorts of conversations adults liked to delude themselves into thinking college students were always having, despite the fact that they had once been college students themselves.

Few were more solemn than me. I had spent the previous days in a torpor, reflecting on my impending failure and unsure of how to prevent it. Though I take pains not to trumpet the fact, I never had to study to get by in school. From those who must spend hours each night poring over textbooks and class notes just to scrape by, I expect little in the way of sympathy. Nevertheless, when the going gets tough and natural faculties and good guesswork are no longer enough to allow people like me to pull another Houdini-style escape act, we find ourselves at a distinct disadvantage. I do not know how to "cram". It is simply not in my nature.

Not that such basic skills would have helped me with one of Professor Broadbent's exams. He was one of the rare, modern educators who demanded his students comprehend the subject being taught, and he structured his exams accordingly. "Provide an economic theory for Rome's slide into despotism in the mid-First Century BCE. Cite specific events from the previous two centuries to support your argument and acknowledge any countervailing analyses of those events from the assigned texts for this course." That was the first question (directive, really; the Professor ordered rather than asked) on that morning's exam. Six o'clock in the morning, to be exact. It was the Professor's belief that a person's mind was sharpest just after waking, and he scheduled his finals as early as the college administrators would allow. I could have provided the Professor with a personal, passionate countervailing example to this belief, but Professor Broadbent did not apply the same academic rigor to all matters that he did to Ancient Rome.

And so, I stared down at the page in much the way a Great Dane might study a Ming vase –

intently, no doubt, but limited in appreciation or understanding. Had we been allowed the use of our textbooks I might have been able to string together a series of thoughts that bordered on the coherent, but Broadbent had denied us even that small grace. The class was expected to know the source material by heart, to be able to cite to it from memory. Ten minutes later the page was still blank, and there were two more just like it to go. Panic gripped me; adrenaline flooded my body, coursing through my bloodstream like a school of electric eels set on "high". I grabbed my pen and began to write. I had heard stories of people navigating stressful situations who later possessed no memory of anything they had said or done at the time, but until then I had never experienced it myself. Had someone asked me at that moment if I knew what was happening, I would have assured them I did. But that was true only in the loosest sense. The next thing I was certain of was Professor Broadbent's nasally voice calling, "Pencils down!". All at once, the classroom around me snapped into focus. Looking down at my test paper I saw that it was covered in writing, line after line of text growing diminishingly small and fevered as it approached the end of each page. My eyes were still regaining focus when my exam was swept up in the stack that was being passed across to the end of the row. Papers turned in, we students rose as one and shuffled toward the door like condemned men to the gallows.

Professor Broadbent shouted after us that we were to return at nine o'clock to receive our scores. How anyone could review and grade twenty exams, each with three essay questions, in under two hours was a mystery to me, but one I was too preoccupied at the time to try to solve.

There are few good ways to kill time at seven in the morning. Too on edge to go back to my room and sleep I thought about getting breakfast at The Big Red Diner, but neither greasy food nor coffee sounded appealing to me. Instead, I spent the next two hours traversing campus, making long, criss-crossing paths from one end to the other, tracing a pattern like the spokes of a bicycle's wheel and passing always by the fountain with the bronze statue of Thomas Bartholomew Bradford that stood roughly at the center of everything. Surrounding the fountain on all sides, at a distance of twenty feet or so, were wooden benches. Despite the beauty of the landscape - the rolling, green lawn sloping gently down from the north end of campus, bisected by footpaths, with each section boxed in by intricately maintained shrubberies interspersed with bellflowers and delphinium, culminating near the south gate in a small pond surrounded by paperbark maples, like some grand English garden of the 18th Century – the benches were arranged *inward*, so that any passerby who was tempted to sit for a moment and rest his or her legs was forced to gaze upon the stern visage of Bradford, a second-generation New Englander whose lineage (a faded bronze plaque assured) traced directly back to the Mayflower. Bradford's connection to the college was never made explicit, but it most assuredly involved money. The trustees were no doubt happy to erect a monument in his honor, desperate to claim even the most tenuous relationship to the region's fledgling Puritan aristocracy. I looked up at the statue as I passed. Bradford's eyes peered out over the landscape to the woods beyond campus, a permanent scowl etched on his face, as if the works of men and God disappointed him equally.

As I paced back and forth past the fountain a man sitting on one of the benches caught my eye. There was nothing unusual about his appearance. He looked to be of average height and build, with short brown hair and pale skin. He was dressed appropriately for the season in a tan corduroy jacket and jeans. In his hands was a newspaper, which made small flapping noises against the breeze. What had grabbed my attention was that each time I approached the fountain, no matter which direction I was coming from, the man would invariably be sitting on the bench directly opposite me. Each time I emerged from one of the footpaths into the courtyard he would fold the top of his newspaper down to peer at me, as if reassuring himself that I hadn't disappeared. Then he would straighten the paper again and continue reading.

After the fourth time this happened I was so unnerved that I decided to run a test to make sure the stress of that morning's exam wasn't causing me to hallucinate. First, I left the courtyard and walked halfway down a particular path, then immediately backtracked and reappeared from the same direction I had just departed. Another time, as the fountain was coming into view in the distance, I tiptoed off the edge of the path I was on, snuck behind a large magnolia bush, and emerged into the courtyard from a different path off to my right. In each case, the result was the same – when I arrived at the fountain there was the man again, directly opposite me, newspaper folded and an arch expression on his face, as if he were a parent regarding a child's clumsy attempts to deceive him.

"You should have said something to him," you might be thinking, but what exactly could I say? The problem with confronting someone who's acting crazy is that you inevitably start sounding crazy yourself. I don't mean someone who is ostentatiously crazy, the proverbial raving lunatic on the subway who everyone within earshot can immediately tell departed the world of the sane long ago. What I mean are the subtle eccentrics, the ones who pass through life behind a mask of respectability while manipulating all those who come within their orbit.

My former roommate from freshman year, Thad Walters, was one such person. He used to get a thrill out of getting into crowded elevators and standing at the front of the car, near the doors. Once the doors closed, he would turn around to stare at the people behind him. It was an assignment he had been given in his Intro to Psychology class, one of a series of set pieces where students were asked to violate some normal mode of behavior in a public place and record the reactions they observed, as well as their personal feelings about those reactions. If only that poor, naïve professor had known what sort of budding sociopath he had in Thad.

The elevator exercise was his personal favorite, a rumspringa for the superego. Not content with the basic framework of the thing, he would add his own personal flourishes; he did not so much look at his fellow occupants as leer, his breathing turning heavy and his skin oily-slick with perspiration, slavering like a celibate dog in a roomful of bare, extended legs. It was psycho-sexual derangement too visceral to be contrived. Gazes darted left and right, down to the ground, into the middle distance, anywhere but at the weirdo at the front of the car shedding sparks from his bulbous eyes. On one occasion, a thick-necked alpha male with a chivalrous streak was also in the elevator and called Thad out, telling him matter-of-factly that he was making people uncomfortable and to turn around. Getting no reaction, the man became increasingly angry, voice rising in pitch as he stomped his feet and pointed a trembling finger in Thad's face. The air grew heavy with violence; now it was the confronter who seemed unhinged. When the doors finally opened, the bystanders scurried from the car like rats from a burning ship. "Why do you do that?" I asked him, but he could never really explain, only shrug dumbly and go about his day. Apparently he considered the self-reflection part of the assignment to be optional.

The man on the bench had a similar aura to Thad's. I decided I had enough on my plate and kept walking, back toward Waverly Hall. It was now a quarter to nine, and I preferred milling about for fifteen minutes to being an unwitting subject in some maniac's demented experiment.

Three of my classmates had already formed a line near the door by the time I arrived, like Black Friday shoppers camping out in front of a store. They looked anxious, though I couldn't fathom why; they were the three best students in the class. I alone represented the other half, whose failures had driven me to toe the ground outside Waverly Hall when I could have been at home asleep in my bed, like any self-respecting twenty-something should be at nine in the morning.

I took my place at the back of the line, sharing a tight-lipped nod of recognition with the man in front of me, so slender it was if he'd been constructed from matchsticks. His name was Nerold, I recalled, or at least that's what it sounded like Old Broadbent called him when taking roll at the beginning of class. That formed the extent of our interaction. Nerold turned his expectant gaze toward the door and fidgeted, shifting his weight from one foot to the other, as if any minute Broadbent might burst forth and exclaim the test results to all assembled like a town crier. The chill air hung damp and heavy around us. I shivered, wondering why we were standing outside when a warm hallway awaited us just on the other side of the door. I was summoning the courage to pull a Thad-like breach of etiquette, step around the three in front of me and slip inside, when the line suddenly began to move. Nerold and his brothers-in-excellence marched inside single file, as precisely as a military honor guard, while I scurried after them like the idiot new recruit.

The closer we got to Broadbent's room the more rebellious my legs became, turning heavy and limp like two disobedient dogs struggling against their leashes. Like any good pet owner, I exerted my will and soldiered on, tugging at my shirt collar to release a sudden buildup of heat. My blood crackled and fizzed like a newly poured drink beneath my skin. Rarely in life does one reach a moment of no return, where the infinite possibilities the world once presented to you are boiled down to a simple, binary choice that will irrevocably shape your future and the person you will become. Here was such a moment, and what's more there was nothing more I could do. The outcome had already been decided, sealed in ink and yet completely unknown, like the fate of poor Schrodinger's cat. "The die is cast" – that's what Caesar had said as he led his army across the Rubicon. Too bad that hadn't been a question on the exam, I thought to myself.

When we reached the classroom, a voice that was obviously Broadbent's called out for the first person to enter. "Close the door!" said the voice. "The rest of you wait outside until called!" We recreated our line, down a man now, though more students were filtering in by the second. By the time I reached the front, the line stretched to the end of the hall and around the corner. There was little time to steady my nerves. Each of the people in front of me had been in and out of the room in less than a minute, emerging with the satisfied expressions of those who had had their high expectations fulfilled.

"Next!" bellowed Broadbent, the door swinging open before I had time to catch my breath. I oozed around the doorframe, aware of how sheepish I must have appeared as I tiptoed into the room. The expression on Broadbent's face when he saw whose turn it was confirmed that my apprehension was warranted. A guttural huff issued from his nostrils before I was even halfway to his desk. I knew at that moment that the box had been opened, the cat had been poisoned, and we were both surely dead.

"Sit," said Broadbent, in a way that conveyed he was extending a courtesy to me I did not deserve. "Mr. Block, correct?" he asked, flipping through the stack of exams on his desk.

"Yes, sir."

He arched an eyebrow. "German?"

"Excuse me, sir?"

"Your name," he said, in a tone suggesting his opinion of me had little room left to fall.

"Ah, sorry sir. Yes, sir."

"Germany's history is intimately intertwined with that of Rome. I would think one of Germanic heritage would be more invested in the plight of his forbearers."

"Yes, sir." I hesitated. "I'm not terribly German, sir, to be honest. I don't speak a word of it. Neither do my parents or grandparents. I'm not sure about my great-grandparents. I only met them once when I was really little, but I don't remember them speaking German. I remember them looking

German, if that makes sense. Not that I knew what a German looked like at that age. Or even now, for that matter. That is to say, it would be presumptuous of me to look at a person and think to myself, well, there goes a German. I mean, unless they were wearing lederhosen or a dirndl or something. But you don't see much of that walking down the street, do you? On a Wednesday? Maybe during Oktoberfest, but even then, it's just as likely to be a tourist, isn't it? Still, when I look back in my mind's eye and try to picture my great-grandparents the first thing that pops into my head is, 'German'. Just a trick of the memory, I suppose. Block…it's just a name, really." I looked around the room, as if whatever else I had wanted to say had been misplaced on the floor somewhere; finding nothing, I settled on, "My first name is Edwin."

Professor Broadbent began to speak, then thought better of it and held out my exam. I took it from him, cradling it as one might a piece of roadkill freshly scooped from the pavement, and looked down, deciding it best to rip the bandage off all at once.

As I contemplated my now-certain fate I heard Broadbent ask, "Do you know what that is?"

I nodded. "It's a 38, sir."

"A failing score," said Broadbent. "Not only failing, but the lowest score of anyone in this class."

He drummed his fingers on the desk and looked toward the window, as if seeking commiseration from the ancient maple standing just outside. "Not the lowest score out of all the classes I teach, however." He retrained his gaze on me, his expression something between curiosity and pity. "I suppose that's of some solace to you?"

"Yes, sir. I mean, no sir." I shook my head. "I'm very disappointed in myself."

Broadbent took a deep breath. Hunched over his desk, lips creased beneath his ample proboscis, he resembled a mole that had reached its wits' end. "It is commensurate, is it not, with the amount of attention and effort you put into your studies?"

"Yes, sir."

"There was no mix-up?" he continued. "In this 38 percent you see no cosmic injustice done to you, no cruel subversion of academic norms?"

"Um…"

Broadbent studied me for a moment, as if wrestling with an idea. Unable to pin its shoulders to the mat, however, he simply nodded, gestured to the door and said, "Good day, Mr. Block." I stood as Broadbent hunched back over and began rifling through his stack of exams like some elaborate, antique card shuffler, feeling like I should say something but having no idea what. The next thing I knew

I was at the door, and the next student in line was being beckoned into the classroom.

That's what put me on a bench outside Waverly Hall at just after nine in the morning, the duality of my theoretical future having given way to the sad, singularity of my present reality. I was a failure. It's one thing to suspect that you're a failure, but to have it documented and certified by a bona fide seat of learning is a psychic shock from which it isn't easy to recover. I had imagined this moment hundreds of times throughout the previous month. One would think I would have been prepared, would have steeled myself for the moment of confirmation and had some sort of plan – a rough sketch at least, or even a sloppy etching – of where to go next. But don't we all harbor a glimmer of hope, even in our darkest hours, that somehow things will turn out ok? Aren't we all to some extent true believers, adherents to a secular faith that things will just "work out" in the end? But now that I had seen it, that '38' scrawled in blood-red ink across the top of my test, a final judgment unassailable in its mathematical certainty, I felt failure's full brunt like a blow to the sternum. I sat there as dazed and hollowed out as any cult member who'd been shown once and for all that their leader was a fraud.

If only I sit here on this bench and don't move, I'm still a student. This is a morning like any other morning. I could stay here the rest of my life and nothing would change. Perhaps that's what I was thinking as I sat and stared at the sky and the dewy lawn and the leaves scuttling down the walk. If so, it was not consciously. I wasn't conscious of anything until I became aware of a person sitting beside me. When I looked to my left, I saw that it was the man in the tan corduroy jacket I had encountered by the fountain.

He clutched the same newspaper as before, bowing his head over it in a bad impression of reading. He had obviously been watching me from the corner of his eye. No sooner had I glanced over at him than he straightened, folded up the paper into a neat rectangle and stuffed it under his arm with the crisp movements of a Marine Corps drill team member. There was a moment where we just sat there, studying one another. I admit to being startled at first, but the man's expression contained a certain conspiratorial glint, completely unrequited on my part, that rendered him too cartoonish to fear. A beatific smile spread across his face. He nodded slowly, as if we'd just come to some profound agreement.

"Who was it?" he said.

I waited for him to elaborate. When it was clear that he wouldn't, I said, "Who was what?"

"That failed you," he said. "Which professor was it?"

I squinted at him and reflexively glanced back toward the door of Waverly Hall. “How did you know I failed?”

“No, no,” he said, shaking his head. “You didn’t fail. They failed you.” He chuckled, stretched his arm out and laid it across the top of the backrest, sinking into the bench as if it were a favorite recliner. “Trust me when I say this place has nothing to offer you.” He brought his leg up to rest on the opposite knee. His pant legs, I noticed, were several inches too short. Black-and-tan checkered socks dotted with holes protruded from his frayed tennis shoes.

“Look,” I said, “no offense, but I have no idea who you are. So, if you don’t mind…” I started to get up, but the man put his hand to my chest with a calm persuasiveness I obeyed almost without thinking. I settled back into my seat.

“I want to tell you a story,” he said. “It’s about a boy, born into a Midwestern family of factory workers just before the time Reagan took office. Back when we could still delude ourselves into believing our lives would turn out even better than our parents’. He was the second boy, soft and round-cheeked, waddling after his bigger brother with a puppy’s dumb grin plastered on his face. Soon there would be a little girl, born two years later, making him the middle child. His parents named the girl Daphne, a “D” name, just like her big-big brother,

David. Her just-big brother, though, was called Barry – Barry Blankenship. When Daphne was a baby, she called him "BB", and the name stuck.

The Blankenship kids had a typical upbringing, as that term is understood in most of America. They were not wealthy. As adults they could spin a yarn or two about their childhoods that had the whiff of hardship about them, but they never truly lacked for anything. They had a house, a modest Cape Cod that was cramped when they were all still living in it, but later became "cozy" when described through the hazy lens of nostalgia. The house was on a street lined with similarly sized houses that varied in style (a Cape Cod here, a craftsman there), but when added together spoke to a singular narrative of post-war prosperity. Their street was one of many named for a common tree type (Ash) that crisscrossed one another and formed the boundaries of a quiet neighborhood off the side of Route 2A, the state road that took you into town (where it changed its name to Main Street) if you headed in one direction, or to the neighboring village, Lumberton, if you headed in the other. It was in this particular corner of a small town called Curwen Falls that the Blankenship children came of age.

The year they turned five, the children of Curwen Falls enrolled in the local elementary school and entered kindergarten, where they would be introduced to the other kids they would call their classmates for the next 13 years. Curwen Falls had only one elementary school, which fed into its one middle school, which in turn fed into its only high school, the utilitarian-named Curwen Falls High. If one were a stickler for exactitude, there was also the Catholic school, Saint Eligius Academy, a squat concrete structure protruding like a malignant growth from the back of the church of the same name. But the students who went to Saint Eligius were a strange and insular bunch, simultaneously looked down upon yet derided as elitist by the public-school families, and as the Academy graduated less than a dozen students in a good year it did not factor into the Blankenship's development in any significant way.

Through elementary school David suffered the misfortune of being an older sibling. He was only two years BB's elder, and once he had entered second grade and BB had begun kindergarten, David did not have a moment to himself. Anytime they were not in class, whether in the halls or on the playground, BB would trail after David, intruding on his games, invading his personal space and embarrassing him in front of his friends.

But as the years passed and they reached that age where cruelty seems to develop in boys as naturally as acne or body hair, the misfortune became BB's. On his first day of sixth grade, not ten minutes after orientation had finished and his teacher, Ms. Willoughby, had introduced herself and gone over the class rules, BB was accosted in the hallway by David and a group of his friends. Too shocked and confused to cry out, BB hung limply as he was lifted into the air by his belt and collar, marched down a little-used corridor that led to the boiler room, and dumped head first into a garbage can containing the remnants of school lunches, worksheets, pencil shavings, and other substances too disturbing to recount. For the next hour BB squirmed and struggled to extricate himself, trying to call out for help while avoiding ingesting any of the putrid mess through which he now pawed like a foraging raccoon.

Finally, Ms. Willoughby grew so concerned about BB's absence that all available faculty and maintenance crew were mobilized, and a sweep of the school was performed. Eventually BB was discovered and hoisted from the can by Mr. Todd, the wrestling coach, and Gene, the head janitor. They took him to the principal's office to get cleaned up and to question him about who it was that had stuffed him in there to begin with. They asked nicely at first, evincing concern and sympathy for what the young boy had gone through, but when it became clear that BB had no intention of ratting out the culprits they became impatient and their voices took on a menacing edge. BB stuck to his story – it had been a group of older boys, though BB did not recognize them and hadn't gotten a good look at their faces. Denied their opportunity to exact vengeance they took their frustrations out on BB, issuing him a demerit for "skipping class" and ordering him to stay after school for the remainder of the week.

It would not be the last time he would suffer because of his older brother. Whereas other sixth graders tiptoed nervously through the hallways wondering if this would be the day when they drew the attention of some sadistic eighth grader whose mission it would become to make the younger boy's life a living hell, BB's fate was sealed right from the start. Once it became clear to David that BB would never tell on him, no matter how badly he and his friends tormented the boy, they thought of little else than new ways to torture him. Whether it was sneaking the recently crushed remains of a frog into his sandwich, holding him down to rub hot sauce on his eyes and lips, or just one of the many shoves, punches or kicks they inflicted upon him as they passed in the hall, David and his friends wasted no opportunity to extract pleasure from BB's suffering.

Nor were things any better at home. One of David's favorite pastimes on lazy afternoons when there was nothing to do (which, to BB, seemed like every afternoon), was to chase his younger brother through the streets of their neighborhood, plinking the backs of his legs with shots from his air rifle. BB would be lying on the couch leafing through a book, when suddenly from across the house David would whoop, "Some BBs for BB!", and BB would know to get up and start running as fast as he could.

After more than a month of such suffering, BB had had enough. He would never tell his teacher or Principal Jeffords what was happening. BB had been raised in a union household. A man never cried to management to solve a problem he could handle himself. But he had been pushed past the limits of even the toughest sixth grader's endurance, and so he went to his father and told him everything about what David had been doing to him – the insults, the shoves, the hitting, the humiliation – the words pouring out faster and faster as he spoke, until they began mixing with the tears streaming down his face and he collapsed in a heap on the floor. Clyde, BB's father, sat in his usual chair at the kitchen table and gazed solemnly out the window, as inscrutable as a sphinx. The worst of the crying passed. BB's sobs slowed to sniffles as he looked up from where he lay; slowly, he lifted himself off the ground and then got to his feet, all the while studying his father who sat like a wax sculpture, illuminated by the late-afternoon sun filtering in through the blinds. The dust motes hovering in the air gave the scene a washed-out look, like a photograph disintegrating with age. His words falling on deaf ears, BB sat silently beside the old man, knowing for certain at that moment that he was on his own.

Clyde had started out in the coal mines. By the summer of his 13th year he was helping out with odd jobs – delivering supplies to the miners, wading up to his neck in muddy water to ensure the pumps were working, cleaning the heavy equipment, but mostly shoveling ton after ton of coal onto the belt line. By 16 he was a red hat and underground with his father, picking up skills here and there and generally doing whatever needed to be done – basic electrical work, roof bolting, driving the shuttle car, repairing the conveyor belt, running the scoop…but still, mostly shoveling. The shoveling never seemed to stop, and no matter how long he kept at it Clyde's arms and back never got used to the strain. His muscles grew hard and ropy and his skin clung to his body as if vacuum-sealed, no slackness or ounce of fat to be seen. This, when added to his pronounced jaw and youthful looks not yet ravaged by his time underground, made him extremely attractive to the young girls in town, including one in particular who would eventually become BB's mother.

All in all, it was a typical upbringing for a boy of Clyde's time and place. The real tragedy of BB's father, however – and thus what became his entire family's tragedy – was that he had a mind, half-smart but endlessly curious, a restless mind unquenched by the dull sameness of his surroundings. When he was a young boy he had sought out books wherever he could find them, a habit so out of place in Pathfork, the small Kentucky town where he grew up, that his own father – BB's grandfather, a hard-bitten scarecrow of a man who looked as if he had been stitched together from cowhide, sinew and scar tissue – would take the belt to Clyde, lashing him across the backs of his legs until the bruises that formed there swelled and burst. But Clyde was hard-bitten himself, a child of a different time and place, and so rather than stop reading as he had been told he simply bandaged up his wounds and found better hiding spots for his books, taking great pains to make sure no one was around before cracking open a cover.

Nevertheless, children being children, he would eventually get careless and be caught again. Then his father would get really angry. "I'll show you!" he'd bellow, and this time he'd attach the big, bronze belt buckle he'd been given by the United Mine Workers for his part in the Harlan County War and wail away on the poor, quivering child balled up on the ground as if it were Herndon Evans himself who lay there. "Read the goddamn words etched in your hide!" his father would hiss, flecks of spit spraying from between clenched teeth. Clyde would absorb it all, thinking only of where he could hide himself next time so that no one would ever find him. There were few less suited to the circumstances into which they had been born than Clyde Blankenship, and no matter how much grim stoicism he projected throughout his life he could not prevent the sickness inside him from eventually infecting the entire household.

It had taken Patty some time to see it. Patty was BB's mother, but before that she had been a pretty Irish girl with dark brown hair who went to Clyde's school. By the time Clyde was down in the mine she worked the counter at the Sunrise Diner. The Sunrise was where most miners went to grab a bite right before or after a shift. Situated as it was across Highway 72 from the dirt road leading up to the mine's entrance, it was perhaps inevitable that they would claim it as their own. But the food was good too, and the owner – a mine widow herself – made the portions extra big for "her boys".

The first time Clyde went into the Sunrise he nearly froze when he saw Patty standing there in her dress and apron, wiping down the countertop with a wet rag. It was the first time he had seen one of his classmates outside of school. He felt strangely embarrassed encountering her like this, a feeling made all the worse by the way some others in his crew spoke to her, things far too sexually aggressive for men his father's age to be saying to a 16-year-old girl. But Patty gave it right back to them, batting her eyes and grinning sweetly as she insulted their manhood, appearance, hygiene, penis size, ancestry, and every other personal characteristic one could think of, employing language Clyde never would have imagined the prim and rather shy girl who sat beside him in homeroom would have known, much less wielded so proficiently.

From that day forward he never saw her the same way again. When the rest of his crew got up to leave, Clyde made an excuse and stayed behind. The Sunrise was mostly empty after the between-shift rushes ended. Clyde walked over to the counter and sat down on one of the stools. Years later, when recounting to BB the story of how she had met his father, Patty claimed that Clyde had said something terribly sweet to her, something that had made her fall in love with him instantly and know at that moment they would be married someday. But neither she nor Clyde could remember what it had been. BB was fairly certain his father had not said anything more romantic than, “Hello”. In truth, they were fated to be together. Two attractive young people living in the same small town with a desperate desire to escape will always end up finding each other. The two of them sat and talked deep into the night, right up until it was time for Patty to clock out and go home. Within a year Patty was pregnant with her first child, and Clyde's father was pulling him out of school to work in the mines full time.

Clyde and Patty were married at Immanuel Baptist Church not long after Patty found out she was going to be a mother. No actual shotguns were used, but it was clear to both kids that there were no other options available to them. The same night Patty left the doctor's office her father sat down with Clyde's father around the former's kitchen table and settled the matter then and there. The wedding would be held as soon as possible, before Patty started showing. Being a miner himself, Patty's father approved of Clyde leaving school to go to work. "My grandkids *will* be cared for," he said, and Clyde's father, who had no use for school as it was, agreed. Having settled the most important matters without incident the rest of the details fell into place like clockwork. Patty would continue to live at home for a few months after the birth, so her mother could watch the baby and give her time to recover. After that, Patty and Clyde could move into the house where Clyde's Great Aunt Celia used to live, a pretty clapboard thing built prior to the Civil War, tucked back into the trees on a small hill on the outskirts of town. It was exactly two months after Clyde's 18th birthday that the young couple stepped over the threshold of their new home, married with a young son and more tied to Pathfork than ever before.

There was a novelty, familiar to all couples if they're able to travel back far enough in their minds' eyes, that made the beginning of this period together the most thrilling and happiest of their lives. Every mundane task, from eating breakfast to greeting one another with a kiss when Clyde returned from the mines in the evening, carried with it a sense of discovery. They felt giddy, almost as if they were children playacting what they thought adults were supposed to do. In David – a healthy, babbling baby now, with all the joys and demands that entailed – they had a shared purpose, a responsibility more solemn than any they had encountered in their lives to that point. They lived together, laughed and cried together, fought (but never for too long) and slept together. Strangely, it was the freest Clyde had ever felt.

What happened then, you ask? Maybe like the scars on the backs of his legs, Clyde's curiosity, his need to discover what more the world had to offer, never completely faded. One evening, about two years after they had moved into Aunt Celia's house together, Clyde returned home from the mines, kissed Patty hello, patted David (who tottered around now on unsteady legs) on the head, and announced that he was taking the following day off of work. Patty had assumed he wasn't feeling well and told him to lie down while she made him some soup. But

Clyde was feeling fine. He reached into his jacket and produced a folded-up piece of paper, which he gave to her. Patty opened the paper and looked at it.

"What is it?" she asked.

"A flier," said Clyde. He had taken it from the bulletin board at the Sunrise Diner. Patty gave him a look; she had been wondering why he was so late getting home. But Clyde waved her off and pointed to the flier again. "I want to go," he said.

Patty looked at him quizzically, then back down at the piece of paper in her hands. "The End of Everything," she read, "America's Apocalypse Obsession and Moral Imperatives in Times of Crisis. Part of the University of Kentucky's Summer Lecture Series." She looked up at him again. "You want to go to *this*?"

"It sounds interesting," said Clyde, moving past Patty to the refrigerator. He took out the milk and started drinking from the carton.

"I've never seen anything like this at the Sunrise before," said Patty. "Where'd it come from?"

"I told you, it was on the bulletin board."

"Who put it there?"

Clyde shrugged. "How should I know, Pat?"

Patty frowned and pointed to the milk carton still in Clyde's hand, now smeared with soot. "How many times have I told you not to touch anything till you get cleaned up?" She ushered him down the steps to the basement shower, reading over the flier again while he washed. It was just as baffling the second and third time through as it had been the first. There was no reason, she had to admit, for her to object. Most women had to deal with their husbands staying out till all hours of the morning drinking, but Clyde was home every night right after his shift ended, like clockwork. How could she begrudge him this one request? And a lecture, no less, at UK. Still, she couldn't help feeling uneasy. Her inability to pinpoint the reason why bothered her. It made her feel petty, self-centered. The best she could come up with as Clyde reemerged, still damp and noticeably whiter than before, was how long of a drive it was. "Nearly three hours," she said. "Two and a half," said Clyde, grinning, and he knew that he had her permission.

The following morning Clyde woke up at his leisure, a thing he had not been able to do in a long time. He took his time getting ready, played with David for a while, then sat down for a long lunch. Finally, as morning shifted into afternoon, he grabbed his keys, kissed Patty and David goodbye and climbed in his truck. Patty stood at the top of the driveway, holding David with one arm as she shielded her eyes from the sun with the other and watched him back out onto the road. With a honk of the horn he drove off in the direction of the highway, then onward, due north toward Lexington.

It was after midnight when the glow of headlights illuminated the living room and woke Patty, who had fallen asleep on the couch. She stood, stretched, and was just shuffling into the kitchen as Clyde walked through the door. "Walked" may have been an understatement; he seemed to float across the linoleum, more buoyant and brimming with life – even at this late hour – than she had seen him since the earliest days of their marriage. "How was it?" she asked sleepily.

"Hey!" he said, as if just noticing she was there. "What are you doing up?"

She shrugged and moved closer to him, pressing against his chest as he encircled her with his arms. "Did you have a good time?" she said, feeling his chin tap, tap, tap against the top of her head as he nodded. "Honestly, Pat," he said, "it was incredible. I never heard anything like it."

"Was it just people talking?"

"Yeah," he said. "But it wasn't like any conversation I ever heard before. The things they were saying…" He inhaled deeply, as if he would need the surplus oxygen to recount all that he had experienced. "It's hard to explain. It's like everything they talked about instantly made sense to me. Almost like they were my own thoughts, only I never had the words to be able to think about it the right way." He paused. "It's like, everything they were saying, they're things that I always sensed about the world, about life. The moment they started explaining an idea, I *knew* it to be true. Only no one ever asked me about it before, so I never had the chance to think about it that way. Do you see what I mean?"

"I think so," said Patty, afraid that she didn't see at all.

"It's like here", said Clyde, "all anyone talks about is the mine or football or their family or who they owe money to. And that's all fine, but then there are these bigger things that people here probably think about to themselves when they're alone sometimes, only we don't ever talk about them with each other. We don't have the vocabulary we need to even be able to think about them the right way."

He stopped, words having failed him once again, and looked to Patty for any sign of understanding. For what it's worth, Patty thought she had a pretty good idea what he was getting at. What he described sounded a lot like being a woman. People talked to you as if you were a child, or worse. Many of the things men had said to her over the years would never be uttered in the vicinity of a child, although on reflection she had been almost a child herself when those sorts of comments had started being directed her way.

The other women in her life talked incessantly about men. The younger ones talked about which men they wanted to sleep with, while the older ones lectured the young ones that they needed to get married, the sooner the better. Now that she herself was married, with a child to boot, she thought maybe the conversation would begin to change, that she and the other married women – content in having achieved the *ne plus ultra* of womanhood – could begin to forge relationships around things beyond the men in their lives. But she was deeply disappointed. The window merely shifted. Instead of talking about the men they wanted to sleep with or marry, they complained about their boorish husbands and all the younger women those husbands chased after. That Clyde not only thought about things beyond the petty scheming that constituted life in Pathfork but wanted so desperately to talk about those things with *her* was the reason she had fallen for him utterly that first night. And yet, there was something bittersweet about his opening up to her like this. She could see he was not happy. Neither was she in a lot of ways. Where Clyde was concerned, however, her joy was unwavering. Was his, she wondered? She knew that he loved her, but how long before the unhappiness he felt, that feeling of being stuck, was transferred onto her and their son? Looking into his eyes now she saw no reason to fear, yet the feeling remained. She leaned forward and kissed him on the lips. "I understand," she said.

Two weeks later, Clyde returned from work with another flier from UK. This one was for a lecture titled "The Colors of the Universe: What Color Can Tell Us About Existence". That was followed by a third lecture discussing some mathematical formula and how it had revolutionized space exploration. Patty had stopped committing the names of the lectures to memory. Whatever profound insights they might have offered were lost in Clyde's increasingly tortured translations. The less able Clyde was to convey the things he had learned, the more committed he became to immersing himself in ever more difficult subject matter. He had something to prove. Patty could see that. She was only mildly surprised at his answer when a large manila envelope arrived for him in the mail one day, and she asked him what it was.

"Study materials," he said. "I'm going to earn my GED."

Well, thought Patty, that was all right. If you ever wanted to work anywhere but the mines, you were going to need a diploma or a GED. Patty gave him a hug and told him that was great news. In the evenings, after Clyde had dragged himself home from work and David had fallen asleep, Patty would make them both coffee and quiz Clyde late into the night, until even the caffeine wasn't enough to keep their eyes from drooping shut. Patty understood much of the material in the study guide; she probably could have passed the exam herself. But the pace at which Clyde improved over the course of their study sessions, the amount of information he retained, was staggering to her. She had underestimated him. It was thrilling to hear him answer correctly a question she hadn't even understood. It turned her on, these displays of knowledge. To encourage him when they went over the more advanced stuff she would sometimes do a striptease – one piece of clothing removed for every correct answer. And when the last piece of clothing had been removed, well…things progressed, as they naturally do. It was during one of these late-night study sessions that their second child – that is to say, I, BB – was conceived.

The test itself was anticlimactic. By the time Clyde had plunked down his $30 registration fee and driven to the town library to take the test, the result was a foregone conclusion. The scores arrived in the mail a few weeks later – no less than 160 on any of the individual tests, and a total score of 720. Clyde was the equivalent of a high school graduate. He waved the paper proudly in front of Patty, like a peacock displaying its feathers. Then they got David and piled in the truck to go out and celebrate. At Shades Café they ordered the most expensive steaks on the menu, drank to their hearts' content and spoke loudly and passionately about every topic that came to mind, animated by that feeling that arises in moments of accomplishment, when life seems to have a direction and purpose toward which you are being unwaveringly propelled.

It was a moment Patty would hold in her heart for years afterward, one of those blissful, too-brief snapshots that are over before you've even begun to appreciate them. Life intercedes, the days drag on and the afterglow fades. Not a month later, Clyde's grumblings started again. First it was frustration with the bosses at the mine. That wasn't so strange. All the guys complained about the bosses. Then it progressed to the vagaries of small-town life. Everywhere you go you run into someone you know, he complained. People are always in your business. He seethed when he couldn't find a single store in the county that sold an air conditioner and had to drive nearly fifty miles to purchase one. When there was a nasty thunderstorm that knocked out their electricity it took the power company three days to get things up and running again, a delay that Clyde attributed to "typical backwoods bullshit". Again, these were frustrations Patty shared, but Clyde's vehemence, the intensity with which he railed against everything associated with Pathfork, spoke to something deeper.

It came out one evening over dinner – a tense, largely silent occasion of the sort that had become more and more commonplace in recent weeks. Patty was fussing with David, trying to get him to eat some of the mashed peas she was spooning toward his face and glancing over at Clyde, who sat staring down at his plate. Suddenly, without looking up, he said, "I applied to college." His words hung in the air. The silence that followed lasted for what felt like minutes, the room frozen like a tableau. Only David craning forward to hazard a bite of his mushy, green dinner, which he abruptly spit onto the tray in front of him, spurred his parents into motion.

"You did?" was the best Patty could manage. Clyde sighed and let his face slide down into his hands. "I'm not angry or anything!" Patty hurried to explain. She didn't know what she was, to be honest.

"Doesn't matter," he said. "I didn't get in." He tossed an envelope onto the table. Patty reached over and slid it the rest of the way toward her. Then she gingerly picked it up, as if it contained a bomb or some poisonous animal, and pulled out the folded sheet of paper inside. The letterhead included an ornate crest – a shield shape containing a cross, images of an open book and a sun's rays, and a banner on which was written text that Patty assumed was Latin – rendered in gold leaf. "Braithwaite College," she read. "Where is that?"

"New Hampshire," he said, absently.

"I…" Patty paused, trying to take everything in. "What made you pick this school?"

Clyde shrugged. “All the best schools are in New England.”

“I never even heard of Braithwaite College.”

“It’s not Harvard or anything. Not an Ivy League school. Maybe a rung or two down.” He chuckled mirthlessly. “I thought I was being *modest* when I applied there. Setting my sights realistically.”

“You never told me you wanted to go to college,” said Patty. When he didn’t respond, she said, “What would we do in New Hampshire? For money, I mean?”

“Guess I figured I’d worry about getting in first,” he said. “Then I’d figure out the money part.”

“Kind of an important part,” she said. “Why not Kentucky? What about UK?”

“I’m done with Kentucky.”

“Oh?” Patty could feel the heat rising in her face. “That’s a pretty big decision to have made without consulting your wife. They have coal mines in New Hampshire?”

“I’m done with the mines, too.”

Patty smacked the table with the palm of her hand, so suddenly and with so much force that it seemed to catapult Clyde and his chair halfway across the kitchen. It startled her almost as badly as it did him. There had been no thought behind it, just uncorked rage spilling from her like lava. Now that it had been loosed, she made no effort to bottle it up again. "GODDAMMIT!" she roared. David began wailing, but Patty ignored him. She rose from her chair and advanced on Clyde, her index finger leveled at him like some accusatory divining rod. "You…don't…GET to be done with the mines!"

Clyde squirmed and backpedaled away from her, as if her finger were a loaded gun aimed at his head. Every inch further that he withdrew, Patty advanced in kind. "I am your WIFE!" she said, then pointed at David. "That is your SON!" Clyde's chair collided with the kitchen sink. He had run out of room. Patty took two more steps, until she hovered over him like an avenging angel. "I know that you're hurting," she said, her voice barely above a whisper. "I know that this life you've been given is not what you would have chosen for yourself. But…" She leaned down low, her eyes inches from Clyde's. "You…*will*…take care of your family. You…"

And then he struck her. The back of Clyde's hand caught Patty across her jaw and froze her mid-sentence. It had happened so quickly that neither Patty nor Clyde seemed certain it had been real. They remained still for several seconds, expressions blank, as if unsure how to proceed. When the spell finally wore off Patty tried to continue, but the spirit had left her. She looked suddenly exhausted, chest rising and falling in steady rhythm despite the trembling hand she placed there to restrain it. Taking a few steps back she continued staring at Clyde, but with softer eyes now, a hundred silent pleas etched in her face. All the anger had drained from her body, leaving her looking diminished and frail.

It would be ungenerous to deny that my father felt many things at that moment – guilt for having deceived my mother, pity for her reduced state, shock at the anger that had been percolating there just below the surface, and embarrassment that he could not look her in the eye and offer an honest defense of himself. And yet, despite all that and despite Clyde's disdain for Pathfork, it was the place of his birth. Its ways and customs were embedded in his marrow, as intrinsic to who he was as the shape of his face or the color of his eyes. Seeing that the fire in my mother had been extinguished, he slowly uncoiled himself, rising from his chair to stand perfectly erect, shoulders back and head held high. To Patty he looked like he was ten feet tall, a colossus advancing across the room toward her with terrifying inevitability. I don't know whether she thought to run. Perhaps she tried, but couldn't. Maybe she saw no need to flee, my father having never given her reason to do so before. There's no telling what went through her head or what she thought my father was capable of. I, of course, not having been born yet and having pieced together my account of this time from the fragments others have let slip over the years, can only speculate.

But what is certain is that when he reached the spot where Patty waited, stooped over and hugging herself tightly, he paused for a moment until she raised her eyes to look at him. Then, without hesitation, he removed his belt and in one sweeping motion lashed her across the face with all of his strength.

The blow sent her sprawling onto the floor. The ones that followed left her curled up in a ball, trembling uncontrollably as she tried to shield herself. After what felt to her like an eternity (but was probably no more than a minute), there was a pause. As the flashes of light began to clear from her eyes Patty dared to uncover her face and look up, only to see Clyde advancing toward her again. She let out a sob and crawled toward the kitchen table for shelter, begging him to spare her. He strode up to the edge of the table until he loomed over her, and she braced herself for the beating to resume. But it didn't. Whether it was the pitiable sight of his wife cowering beneath him or something else that dampened his rage, Clyde suddenly went blank, like a sleepwalker coming to in the middle of one of their late-night forays. Blinking his eyes, he staggered backwards until he no longer straddled Patty, moving his mouth as if to speak but making no sound. Then he wandered out of the kitchen, through the house and into the backyard, where he remained the rest of the day. He was still there when Patty went to bed that night. She lay awake, listening for the sound of the front door that would tell her Clyde was on his way to the bedroom. At first she dreaded it, the thought of him sliding under the covers to press against her. But as the hours passed and the house remained as still as a cemetery, she grew anxious and wondered what was keeping him. The more she worried the more tired she became, until at last her body shut down and she fell into a heavy, dreamless sleep.

It was half past nine the following morning when she awoke. She couldn't remember the last time she had slept so late. Sounds of life emanated from the other room. For a moment she panicked, thinking David was alone wandering through the house unsupervised, but the noises she heard were too purposeful and self-assured to be made by a toddler. Clyde had not run off after all.

Patty climbed out of bed and hurried to get dressed. She went over to her makeup table and quickly touched up her face, concealing the worst of the previous night's damage. The ritual steeled her for the confrontation to come. Looking in the mirror, she took a deep breath and ran through all the things she would say to him, all the possible scenarios for how this morning would play out. When she had finally gathered up the courage to leave her room, to look Clyde in the eye and deliver the lines she had so carefully prepared for him, she strode through the door, only to be confronted by a sight that made her immediately forget everything.

The living room and kitchen were littered with cardboard boxes – some empty, others packed to varying degrees with things from around the house. Still others were taped shut and waiting by the side door, which was propped open. While she was taking all this in, Clyde came inside. He barely spared her a glance as he grabbed the nearest box and carried it back out with him. Patty moved through the room until she had a view of the driveway. Clyde was hoisting the box up into the bed of their pickup, already half-filled with other boxes strapped in place with rubber bungee cords. When he was finished, he returned to the kitchen to get the next box, intent on his task and giving no indication he saw Patty standing just a few feet away.

Patty tried to reconstruct all the things she had wanted to say to him, but the words would not come. "You're leaving?" was all she could manage.

Clyde sorted through the taped boxes, lifting each one an inch off the ground to test its weight. "No, we're leaving."

"What do you mean *we're* leaving?" said Patty.

"You, me and David. The whole family."

"Now hold on a minute…"

Before she could finish Clyde came around the boxes and strode toward her, a terrible purpose in his step and the same glassy expression on his face as when he'd beaten her the evening before. What had seemed an aberration then now came so naturally to him. Patty flinched and raised her arms protectively as Clyde advanced within an inch of her. "I just…!" she said. The room was silent, save for her quick, shallow breathing. Finally, she lowered her head and nodded, mumbling her assent and knowing then that she had missed her moment. Clyde hesitated, as if unsure how to proceed now that he had gotten his way. "Good," he said at last, and told her to start packing up some of David's things.

They made it as far as Pittsburgh, or thereabouts. Some podunk mill town half an hour's drive from the city, along the Monongahela River. Clyde knew a guy there, a cousin of a friend, who said he could get Clyde a job at a powdered metal plant working a press. It was just temporary, Clyde said. They would save a little money, then keep moving east. Always east! That was the grand plan. The East was where learning and culture and respectability resided. If he could just make it there the universe would take care of the rest. He would find whatever it was he was looking for. Then I was born, and Curwen Falls was as far as we got. What followed was years of monotony, loneliness and resentment, until the day I graduated high school and left home for good. My parents were distant, private people. I never saw them smile or show affection, toward me or anyone else. Every happy memory I have of them was told to me by someone else. You know my parents as well as I do now.

Chapter 4

I could tell he was looking for a way to tie things up, but he had run out of words. All he could do was shrug and look to me to pick up the thread.

"So, you're BB," I said. He nodded. "Well, that's quite a story, BB, but I'm not sure what the takeaway is."

"Simple," he said. "This school tore my family apart. My father never got over Braithwaite turning him down. Up until the day he died he kept looking for ways to prove himself." As he spoke, BB scratched incessantly at the corners of his fingernails. A hangnail on his left thumb had begun to bleed. "When my own acceptance letter arrived, I imagined how proud he would have been if he could have seen it, to know that his decision to move us out of Kentucky hadn't been a mistake. His dreams would be fulfilled, if only through his son. But after three years they rejected me too. I got suspended."

"A sad denouement," I said. "But what does any of this have to do with me?"

"Everything. We're going to set things right, you and I."

"How?"

"By stealing the statue of Thomas Bartholomew Bradford."

My feelings about his plan must have been evident, because he immediately said, "Now, hold on…!", as if my reaction were as predictable as it were disappointing. His hands waved about in the space between us, as if any words I might speak were a cloud of bothersome flies to be warded off. Nevertheless, I persisted.

"I…ju…I just…don't…" I said, raising a forearm to parry the hands flapping in my face. "I just don't see the point!"

The point, he said, was retributive. When I told him that revenge didn't appeal to me, he shook his head. "What if I told you," he said, "that everything has already been decided? That you do help me take the statue?" I asked him what he meant. "What if I told you I've seen the future?" he said.

That was my cue to leave. Whatever failings I possess, a dearth of pride is not among them. I stood, told BB he could find some other simpleton to help him with his plan, and said goodbye. I expected him to try to stop me, to clutch at my wrist like a Victorian beggar and plead for me to hear him out. Instead, he just smiled and crossed his arms, saying nothing. With a final half-wave, I started down the footpath toward my apartment. After a few seconds, I paused and turned. BB was right where I had left him, stretched out on the bench and following my retreat with the dozy, self-satisfied expression of a well-fed cat. Annoyed, I turned and stalked away, looking back only when I was sure I had put enough distance between us that he would see he was dealing with a man who meant business. BB stared back at me, his posture unchanged. Determined to get the up-per-hand, I made a silent promise not to look back again as I followed the footpath's long arc all the way around to the opposite side of the quad. When I glanced surreptitiously across the grassy expanse, I could see him in the distance, still sitting there on the bench, as smugly serene as a trust-fund Buddhist.

Five minutes later I was back at Waverly Hall, seated next to him.

"Why are you so confident I'll help you?" I said.

"I told you, I've seen it," he said, matter-of-factly.

"What does that mean?"

"In a dream." Seeing my expression, he said, "Look, I know how that sounds. But the universe sends me messages." He spoke conversationally, as if discussing the weather. "Every time I make a choice the universe reacts. I've learned to read its signals, to use its feedback to inform everything I do." He shrugged. "Anyone can do it, I assume."

What pale sunlight managed to elbow its way through the clouds seemed to collect in BB's pupils, glinting there like tiny stars. "How do you think I found you? I never met you before, had no idea who you were. But I knew I would find you because it was fated. Every choice I've made brought me here, to this place and time. So, I waited and waited for as long as it took. When I saw you I knew you were the one. There was no doubt in my mind that I should ask you to help me, just as I never doubted you would say yes…"

"Who says I said yes?" I interjected.

BB ignored the question. "Now it's time for the two of us to follow the universe's cues."

"The universe wants us to steal a statue of Thomas Bartholomew Bradford?" I said. "Who the hell was he, anyway?"

A Calvinist minister, said BB. During King Philip's War he had helped run the internment camp on Deer Island, earning his salary starving Praying Indians to death. When the war ended, he had snapped up tracts of tribal land in Massachusetts and Rhode Island, selling them off piece by piece over the ensuing decade until he had amassed a small fortune. A real creep, through and through. There was no karmic retribution to be faced for ripping up his statue, BB assured me. The old gods would smile on us. All at once his eyes lit up. "We'll take him with us!" he said. "He'll be our talisman! The spirits of the road will bless our journey!"

"What journey?" I said.

BB put his hand on my shoulder and leaned closer. “There’s nothing for us here. Look around…” Like an actor hitting his mark, BB’s gaze broke from mine to sweep back and forth over campus. Without thinking I followed suit, taking in the same sights that had been so familiar to me for the past four years – Waverly Hall, with Wheelwright Hall beyond that; the footpath, lined with benches nestled in the shade of sugar maples towering overhead; farther down, the faux-Japanese garden with the wooden bridge crossing over a stream that flanked the great, green expanse of the quad. It didn’t feel like nothing, but I knew that it wasn’t mine anymore. “What do you have in mind?” I said.

“We just go.”

“Like that? No plan?”

“When you can’t stay where you are, go someplace else. Just keep moving. Movement is living; the rest is just waiting around to die.”

“You stole that quote,” I said. BB shrugged, a mischievous grin on his face.

“We should forget the statue,” I said, realizing only after I had spoken that I had tacitly agreed to come with him. “You know how much an eight-foot-tall bronze statue must weigh?” BB, though, wouldn’t budge. The statue was a catalyst, he said. Every journey needed a driving force. I pointed out that this contradicted everything he had just told me, but BB just waved his hand. Never had I met a person so certain of everything at once. It was philosophy by whim.

"How do we even get the statue?" I asked him. "How do we take it off the pedestal? How do we transport it?"

BB clapped his hands. He could tell the hook was set. All he had to do was keep reeling. "*That*, I've been planning for."

That morning was not the first time BB had been lurking near the fountain. Every night for the past week he had been reconnoitering the area, keeping a detailed journal in which he had catalogued the names and movements of everyone he observed. There was also a crude schematic he had drawn up that showed the nearby buildings and calculated a potential observer's sight lines depending on what floor they were standing on and taking into consideration the cover provided by nearby vegetation.

According to BB's notes the night watchman (our school was far too small to have its own police force) made three rounds through campus every night, which brought him past the fountain at roughly 12:15, 2:45, and 5:15 in the morning, give or take five minutes. The pattern had remained consistent throughout the week. That was no surprise. Like most students, I knew the night watchman, a creaky, nonagenarian named Soames who was an early alum of the college back when they still accepted graduates of the local preparatory school regardless of family name or wealth. Had he been occupied in any other vocation he would have retired years ago, but the college inspired in him – the son of a brakeman for the Boston and Maine Railroad – a loyalty peculiar to one of the lower classes upon whom the aristocracy had shown grace. Half-blind and ambulatory only in the strictest sense, he would not trouble us.

The town police also patrolled the area, but only by car. Their appearances were less frequent and predictable than Soames's, but the statue was in the center of campus, far from the main roads, and BB was confident we could operate with impunity under cover of darkness. Only the night before, BB had taken it upon himself to shimmy up the lamppost nearest the fountain and remove its bulb. This had acted as a low-stakes test run, (after all, how much trouble could he really get in for tinkering with a light?), and would make their job easier when it came time to steal the statue.

"Won't Soames just notice the lamp is out and come snooping around?" I said.

BB laughed. "He's passed by twice since I swiped the lightbulb and didn't so much as bat an eye. I'm not sure he can tell night from day!"

On and on it went like that – me pointing out some potentially fatal flaw in the operation, and BB rattling off his rebuttal as if he'd been prepped on my objections in advance. He knew the size and type of bolts used to fasten the statue to its base and had pilfered a set of wrenches, pliers (both tongue-and-groove and diagonal), bolt cutters, a hacksaw, and a circular saw from the industrial design center. Most statues are held down by bronze pins, he said, poured over with epoxy glue to hold them in place, but for this statue they had used mounting nuts. And once the statue was loose? The weight was daunting, he admitted – probably about 1,200 pounds. That was that, I figured, but if anything BB grew even more confident, explaining that he had taken measurements and determined that if we backed up a moving truck (he had already rented the truck, he confided; it was stashed off-street in the driveway of a friend who was out of town for the next few days) right up onto the lip of the fountain, the back of the truck would be at a perfect distance and angle that we could simply push the statue until it tipped over, directly into the cargo area. Then we would slam the doors shut, hop in the cab, and drive all night until we were a couple states away.

BB dusted off his hands when he had finished his explanation, effectively declaring the deal to be closed. "Eight o'clock tonight, meet me at the rec center for open gym. Pack only what you need, whatever will fit in a single bag."

We parted then as abruptly as we had come together. I raced back to my apartment, pausing outside my front door for a moment to scan my surroundings before slipping inside. What I was looking for I couldn't tell you, only that my caution seemed justified; the air was charged with some unsettling energy that made even the act of entering my own home feel illicit. Safely inside, I went to my bedroom and began rummaging through the closet for something to pack. No sooner had I opened the door than I spotted a gym bag – a maroon, canvas duffel speckled with the ghosts of sweat stains past – that I hadn't seen since freshman year, when I had briefly flirted with intramural soccer. Inexplicably, it was laid out atop the shoes and other junk scattered across the floor, as if it had somehow known that this was the day it would be called back into action.

That morning's failed exam and my looming suspension were distant memories now. Back and forth I scampered from the closet to the dresser, like a baserunner caught in a rundown. There were nearly nine hours left before BB and I had arranged to meet, yet I felt a sense of urgency, as if the slightest hesitation in my preparations might doom our plan to failure. I went back to the maroon duffel and held it open, stretching it this way and that as if I could increase its capacity through sheer will. In the end I managed to fit two full changes of clothes, an extra pair of socks and sneakers, a toothbrush, and a Swiss Army knife I had received for my 13th birthday and kept hidden away in a junk drawer. My wallet, passport, and any cash I had lying around I stuffed in my pockets.

Once I had finished packing, my nervous energy had no outlet. Like a caged animal, I paced from one end of the apartment to the other, checking the kitchen clock each time I passed. It was not yet noon; still more than eight hours until I was due at the gym. I thought about using some of that time to write a note letting everyone know that I'd gone, until I remembered that I lived alone and there would be no one to read it. My stomach twisted in on itself, a feeling that quickly reimagined itself as hunger. I decided to grab a bite to eat. Putting on my jacket, I slipped out of the apartment and headed back across campus toward the Big Red Diner.

Though there were quicker routes I could have taken, I found myself choosing a path that led past the fountain and the statue of Bradford. Whether it was a desire to scout the location before that evening or just a morbid curiosity that compelled me, I can't say. As I passed the ring of benches and entered the courtyard where the fountain stood, I slowed my gait, sneaking a glimpse at the severe, patrician face glaring out at the horizon, as if beyond it were only new problems to be brought to heel. Something about that face – the hard lines, the inherent cruelty that even the sculptor had been unable to mask, preserved in bronze and towering over all who approached – mesmerized me. No longer trying to conceal it, I stood at the statue's feet and gazed upward like a struck-dumb supplicant, rocking gently to an invisible melody.

Out of the corner of my eye I glimpsed a startled movement. Looking to my left, I saw BB perched on the end of one of the benches. He was arranged just as he had been the first time I had seen him, newspaper held wide as he peeked over the top. He ducked his head down when he realized I had identified him, then slowly raised it again until our eyes met. He blinked at me, then darted his eyes toward an empty spot on the bench to his right, over and over until his message couldn't be clearer. As nonchalantly as possible, I ambled over and sat down, doing my best to look at nothing in particular. For the next minute or so I waited, expecting him to say something. When he didn't, I began to wonder if he had gotten up and left. Just as I was turning to check, a voice hissed, "*Don't look at me!*" My head snapped back.

"*What are you doing here?*" said BB. He kept his voice low, but the venom was unmistakable.

Like a character in a spy movie, I mimicked a yawn, placing my hand over my mouth. "*What?*" I murmured. "*Nothing. Just passing by.*"

"*We shouldn't be seen together. You're going to ruin everything.*"

I pretended to scratch my nose. "*What are you talking about?*"

"*This is the second time today we've been seen together by the fountain. That statue goes missing and they start canvassing for witnesses, who do you think will stand out in most people's minds?*"

He had a point. "*Sorry,*" I whispered. "*I'll go.*"

"*Where?*"

"*The Big Red. I'm going to grab some lunch.*"

"*Meet you there in half an hour.*"

The rustle of BB's newspaper signaled that the conversation was over. I got up from the bench and resumed walking, silently cursing myself for being so careless. Would the plan have to be delayed now, I wondered, or even called off altogether? The rumbling in my stomach made it impossible to brood. I pushed all thoughts from my mind and focused on getting to the Big Red. Once I'd eaten, I could think more clearly.

"Big Red" was the colloquial nickname for Brathwaite College's athletic teams. Given that the teams' uniforms were burgundy and white it was a curious sobriquet. The official team nickname was the "Fellows", an image which struck fear into exactly no one and from which even the Violets of NYU felt no impulse to shrink.

The walls of the Big Red Diner were covered in typical sports memorabilia – pennants and pom-poms and megaphones emblazoned with the school's logo, framed action shots of star athletes from past generations, game balls from historic victories, etc. In a glass case affixed to one of the dining room walls, arranged like a shrine, was a basketball signed by the team that had qualified for the NCAA tournament back in the 1960s. On the other side of the room, like a mirror image, was another case containing a jersey of the one and only player the school's football program had sent to the NFL, a tight end who had played three seasons for the Denver Broncos before retiring to go work for a hedge fund.

It was seat yourself at the Big Red. I picked a booth along the back wall, near the restrooms, and waited for the waitress to come over. The diner was unusually busy for a Wednesday afternoon. Nearly every table was filled with students laughing and carrying on, the whole room abuzz with post-finals euphoria. The men spoke loudly and boastfully, shedding all innuendo from their patter as they propositioned the girls in their company in the most explicit manner imaginable, the girls shrieking in mock embarrassment and giving playful slaps or pinches in return. In the booth adjacent to mine a tall, strapping kid who looked as if he had wandered in straight off the farm hoisted a petite, heavily made-up young girl over his shoulder and carried her squealing toward the restrooms. Those in the vicinity laughed and pointed, while the rest paid no notice at all. It was a day for setting aside social niceties and giving in to excess. The very air throbbed. The floor seemed to rock and sway beneath my feet, as if the building itself were drunk.

When the waitress finally appeared, I ordered a hamburger and cup of coffee. The clock above the kitchen read ten after twelve – 20 minutes until BB was supposed to arrive. As I scanned the room, a familiar face caught my attention. Seated at one of the round tables toward the front of the restaurant was Greta, the girl who had sat next to me and with whom I had flirted in our dreary Revolutionary-Napoleonic Europe course the previous semester. She looked just as I remembered her, her pointy nose and high cheekbones giving her an imperious air that seemed incongruous with the gawky, angular body she still had not fully grown into. Her golden-brown hair, piled haphazardly on top of her head, appeared to glow as it caught the sun's rays angling in through the window behind her.

I stared at her, dumbstruck. We had parted ways with such finality at the semester's end that I had expected never to see her again. That we had not once crossed paths on such a small campus since then only reinforced my belief that she had left school for good. Seeing her now was like encountering a ghost, only more than that. I had expunged her from my memory – every image, every word she had spoken, every moment we had shared – and her sudden reassertion into my life shocked me as deeply and fundamentally as if I had discovered that I possessed a hidden past. Perhaps I watched her too intensely and for too long, because eventually her eyes found mine. After the briefest of pauses her mouth opened and a shudder of recognition passed through her.

My heart began to race as I watched her lean over the table and offer a few hurried words to her companions. I knew she was about to approach me. All at once I found myself to be a collection of unpleasant characteristics. My clothes seemed shabby, better suited for lying around the house than being seen in public. My hair looked as if I had combed it with my fingers. My mouth felt dry, the saliva congealed into a paste that coated my tongue and turned my breath sour. I looked around in vain for my waitress, wishing I had thought to order a glass of water.

Before I knew it, Greta was standing over me. Seeing her up close only deepened my self-consciousness. She was immaculately made-up, her eyebrows penciled in with a painter's care, lashes teased out to draw attention to her warm brown eyes, between which rested a furrow of resentment. Her skin, blushed and polished, emitted a rosy glow beyond the natural, as if she were a figure in a Renaissance painting. Although simply dressed – a snug cotton shirt and a pair of jeans – she would not have looked out of place at a formal gala. She appeared to me the way I assumed movie stars looked in their day-to-day lives, eternally put together, radiating an easy confidence that cannot be learned or imitated. I shrank from her, feeling my shoulders bunch and my gaze drop to the floor even as I tried to prevent it.

"I didn't expect to see you here," she said.

Irritation cut through the nervousness and allowed me to find my voice. "I could say the same to you. How are you, anyway?"

"Fine," she said, gesturing back toward the table she had just left. "As you can see."

I nodded, realizing too late that it was my turn to respond. "I…I haven't seen you in forever."

"I've been busy. You know how it is, finals and everything."

"I didn't even know you still went to school here."

"Still here," she said. She pursed her lips, shifting her weight from one foot to the other. She glanced at the empty seat across from me. “Do you mind?”

“Of course not,” I said, apologizing for not having invited her sooner. I half-stood in a simulacrum of gallantry as she slid into the booth, my nostrils filling with vanilla and sandalwood as her perfume billowed across the table. Slouching back into my seat, I scrambled for anything to say, no matter how banal. “So, what have you been up to?”

She shrugged. “Same as always – studying, working. At least until today.”

“That’s it?” I said. “You’re all done?”

“Last final was this morning.” She cocked her head to the side and for the first time grinned, revealing two rows of unblemished white teeth. “Nothing left to do but get wasted and wait around to collect my diploma. Then I guess it’s off to the real world.”

I chuckled lamely and glanced at the clock – ten more minutes. When I looked back at Greta she was studying me, her mouth creased. It was the same expression my mother used to make whenever I had disappointed her somehow. “What about you?” she said.

“Fine,” I said. “I had my last final this morning too, actually.”

“Great,” she said. I nodded. Greta folded her arms over her lap and began tapping her fingers on her elbow. “So, what comes next?”

“After lunch?”

She rolled her eyes. “Like, after you graduate. Do you have a job lined up, or will you go to graduate school, or…?”

“Greta, how come you never called me?” The words were out before I realized what I was saying. My body clenched as if bracing for a collision, but now that I had started I was powerless to stop. “I thought you were gone. I thought you had moved away or something.”

“Eddie…” she said. I winced. No one else called me Eddie, only Greta. She had started calling me that the first time we met, and I had let her, too polite or shy or smitten to correct her. Its false familiarity bothered me now, its implied insistence that nothing had changed. Greta sighed and shifted in her seat. Something of the glow had left her face. “I don’t know why you would think that. I never said anything about moving.”

“You vanished,” I said.

“I’m here.” She pointed to herself. “I’ve been here the whole time.”

“I haven’t seen you once since we went on break…”

"I…" Greta paused, looking resigned, as if some unpleasant but inevitable thing had finally begun. "I don't know what you want me to say, Eddie. I guess we never crossed paths. It's not like I was hiding away in my room for the last three months."

"The way you said goodbye…" I raised a hand to stop her from interrupting. "No, wait…the way you said goodbye on the steps after class – 'Well, I guess this is it,' you said. As if that's the last time we would ever speak. You never said anything about having another semester here, you didn't say, 'See you after Christmas'…"

"Neither did you," she said.

"I wasn't the one saying goodbye like I was getting on a bus and leaving forever."

"Look, I can't do this…"

"You didn't even give me your number! You never came by to say hello!"

Greta looked around at the neighboring tables, her cheeks turning even pinker than before. "Honestly?" she said. Her eyes narrowed as she faced me. "What did you expect, Eddie? After what happened?" She side-eyed the next table again, leaned in and lowered her voice. "After what *you* did to me?"

I stared at her, too confused to respond. Greta's eyebrows drew together and she glared back, unblinking. "Don't you even…" she hissed.

"Greta, I…"

"Oh, Eddie…" Greta shook her head and averted her gaze, face screwed up like she might start crying at any moment. She held up her hands as if surrendering. "Look, I'm not out for revenge, ok? I'm not going to report you to the school, I'm not going to call the cops. I'm willing to let the past be the past and move on. I could have just ignored you altogether right now, pretended like I didn't see you. But I'm here. I'm willing to talk things over. So at the very least, have the decency not to treat me like I'm an idiot, ok?"

"I'm not!" I said, scrambling to regain some kind of control. I racked my brain, looking for anything to latch onto that would help me make sense of what she was saying. "Look, I…I'm not saying that I didn't…do *something* to hurt you. I just…"

My words trailed off. After a short pause, Greta shook her head. "You have no idea what I'm talking about, do you?" She studied me as if I were some opaque curiosity she'd just unearthed in a foreign bazar. "You don't remember."

Before I could formulate a response, a familiar voice cut me off. "Hello?" it said. I looked over and there was BB in his tan corduroy jacket, a polite grin glued to his face as he leered down at us. He introduced himself to Greta, but she didn't respond.

"Interrupting anything?" he said, in a way that made clear he didn't care one way or the other.

I started scooching over so BB could sit down, but Greta said, "I've got to get going." I tried to talk her into staying, but she brushed me aside before I could finish a sentence. BB was no help, bowing and grinning as he ushered her along. With a final unceremonious wave Greta retreated to the safety of her old table. I watched her for a minute or two, wondering if she would turn and look my way again, but she kept her eyes pointed in the other direction. There were hurried words exchanged with some of her friends, a few of whom shot me icy looks.

All this time BB had remained standing, studying the room with a detached amusement. Finally, he slid in to take Greta's place and fixed me with a wry look. "Who was that?"

"No one," I said.

"A very pretty no one." His voice had a teasing, almost condescending edge. I shrugged.

"Have you slept with her?" he said.

"None of your business."

BB held up his hands, a look of mock offense on his face. "Ok, ok. It was just a question." The waitress came with my food and asked if we needed anything else. We shook our heads. As she left, BB glanced over his shoulder toward Greta's table. One of the others sitting there, a girl in a baggy white t-shirt, her hair tied in dozens of tight braids that protruded from her scalp in all directions like wires from a circuit breaker, scowled and gave him the finger. BB smiled broadly and winked, raised his hand and wiggled his fingers at her. He turned back around and chuckled. "Lesbian," he said. "The one who flipped me off, not your girl. Though maybe she is too, who knows?" He shrugged. "Not you, apparently."

"Can you not be an asshole?" I said. I explained to him about Greta, how we'd met each other and hit it off right away, how we used to make each other laugh during class, whispering running commentaries about Professor Lind to each other as he droned on and on about the Siege of Toulon. How we started taking walks together in the evening when class let out, walks that got longer and longer as the semester went on until we found ourselves wandering campus alone underneath the stars, the only sounds those of our voices and footfalls against the pavement. Then I told him about the last day of class, the way she'd said goodbye as if it were the last day we'd ever see each other, and how I went back to my apartment and sank down on the edge of my bed, just staring at the walls until the sun came up. That was the last time we had spoken until today, when she told me I'd done something that had made her want to cut off all contact with me.

"What did you do?" said BB.

"I don't know," I said. "Honestly, I have no idea."

BB pressed his lips together, looking down at the table as he mulled this over. After a few moments he shrugged and said, "Forget her. She's not important." His expression turned serious. "You need to start focusing." As if to drive the point home, he leaned across the table and jabbed a bony finger into my chest. "What happened back at the fountain, what just happened here…" He gestured over his shoulder toward Greta. "No more. It's happening tonight, Edwin. We've only got about seven hours until this thing kicks off. No more room for mistakes – no hanging out at the scene of the crime, no chasing after pussy you used to know…"

"That's not what that was."

"Is your bag packed?" asked BB. I told him it was. That seemed to placate him a little. "Good," he said. "Now eat up. Once you finish, go straight back to your place and stay there until it's time to meet at the gym. Don't leave for any reason – not for food, not for fresh air, and certainly not for any girl."

I wolfed down my burger while BB rhapsodized about the journey we were about to take. The thing in life was to have choices, he explained. He had spent too long going through the motions that other people had dictated for him. Now he wanted all the choices to be his. "Just me and the universe," he said. "I make a choice, the universe responds and presents me with another set of options, and then I choose again."

"That sounds like regular old life to me," I said between bites.

"Nope." BB shook his head. "Life is passive, mostly. You're told what will happen and you let it happen. That's how it was for me." He reached over and took a fry from my plate. "One day I was cutting through the lawn behind Rose Hall, the one that brings you out on the backside of the student center. I was late for something; I can't remember what. There were a couple textbooks under my arm, very heavy. I think Organic Chemistry was one. Who knows why I didn't have my backpack, but I didn't. I was speed-walking, the way you do when you need to run but can't or are too embarrassed. My arms were burning from the weight of the books. I kept shifting them around to give my muscles a rest. It was early. The dew on the grass had started soaking through my sneakers into my socks. I started cursing to myself. I hate when my feet get wet. All of a sudden, I stopped. I looked around – at Rose Hall, at the woods that separate the highway from campus, at the student center and other buildings in the distance, even down at myself and the books I was carrying. I didn't recognize any of it. I don't know how else to explain it, but nothing I saw made any sense."

The entire time he had been talking BB had been eyeing my plate hungrily. I pushed it toward him and told him to help himself. "Like amnesia?" I said.

He shook his head as he chewed. "No. I knew where I was. I knew *who* I was. I just had no idea how I had gotten there." He paused, as if considering something. "That's when I made my first choice. I disappeared. I didn't even take my books, just dropped them right there in the grass and left."

"I thought you said you were suspended."

"That came later."

"Where did you go?"

"Away." He waved his hand vaguely. "I took some time to think about things. Once I came back, I made my second choice, which was to take the statue."

"Of all the things to choose…"

"Still, it's my choice, and mine alone. And look!" He pointed at me. "The universe responded. It led me to you."

He fixed me with a satisfied smile. There wasn't much I could say to that. I swallowed the last bite of my burger and flagged down the waitress to ask for the check. "Remember," said BB, as we parted ways outside the diner, "don't leave for any reason. Don't even answer the door. Wait until it's time, then grab your bag and head straight to the gym." I promised him I would and returned home, giving the fountain and the statute of Thomas Bartholomew Bradford a wide berth this time.

When I entered my apartment, I immediately locked the door and fastened the deadbolt. Why, I wondered a moment later? BB's paranoia was rubbing off on me. It had been months since anyone had knocked on my door besides the mailman. Nevertheless, I left the locks fastened and returned to the bedroom to double-check my bag. Satisfied I had everything I needed, I wandered out to the living room and sat on the sofa. The clock on the TV stand confirmed what I had feared – six more hours until it was time to go. I grabbed the remote and turned on the TV. When the screen flickered to life, a man in a suit holding a microphone – obviously a local news reporter of some sort – was standing just off the side of a highway. Behind him was a densely wooded area. Somewhere within those woods something was burning. The air glowed varying shades of orange, flickering and changing with the movement of the flames and the lights of the emergency response vehicles that were parked nearby out of frame. Every so often there was a flare-up so violent that the light it gave off cast a glare over the camera lens that made it impossible to see. These lasted only a second or two, accompanied by great belches of smoke that pushed their way free of the forest's canopy to roll upward into the sky.

"...incredibly hot here, Jim," said the reporter. "I've covered many fires over my years here at Channel 8, but I can tell you I have never felt heat this intense from such a distance. You know, you talk about jet fuel and how hot that burns, and of course we all remember on 9/11 the fuel from those planes burning hot enough to *melt* the superstructure of the Twin Towers and cause them to collapse, but to actually feel it now in person is a whole other thing. In fact, uh, the fire chief approached us just a minute ago and advised that we need to clear the area as it may no longer be safe for us to be this close to the flames. I for one am not going to argue, it is *intensely* uncomfortable where I'm standing. We're going to sign off for the moment and send things back to the studio while we pack up and get ourselves to safer ground."

The screen switched over to a studio set where a buttoned-up man with salt-and-pepper hair and a pinstripe suit sat behind a desk beside a well-coifed, heavily tanned woman in a sleeveless dress. "Absolutely, Ron," said the man. "Please stay safe out there, and as always thank you for your report. Again, if you're just joining us, a 737 commercial jet carrying 136 passengers crashed this morning in an area just off of Old Stage Coach Road, about five miles north of Pine Ridge. First responders have been unable to get near the crash site to search for survivors as fire crews continue to battle the intense flames…"

The anchor went on, assuring viewers that they would rejoin their team at the scene of the crash as soon as they had found a safer vantage point from which to report. I waited while the broadcast cycled through local news canon - crime (DUIs mostly), news from the statehouse (budget talks had stalled), the weekend calendar (5k Fun Run for a good cause), and of course the weather (Friday - mild, Saturday - pleasant). There had been something mesmerizing about that brief clip of the crash, the pulsating yellow-orange-red and the smoke billowing out from the trees, as if some great beast of mythology had awakened in the depths of the New Hampshire wilderness and was advancing upon civilization. Meanwhile, my eyelids grew heavier. The female anchor segued into a commercial break, teasing once again that there would be more from the crash site if conditions improved, but the endless procession of pharmaceutical and personal injury lawyer ads that followed proved too much for me to withstand. Vaguely, as if recalling the sensation from memory, I felt the remote slip from my hand. The next thing I knew I was sitting across a desk from a professionally dressed young woman, her black hair pulled back into a bun.

We were in a high-rise office, dozens of stories in the air. A corner office, with windows stretching from floor to ceiling. Outside were other buildings of varying heights reaching toward the sky like weeds jockeying for sunlight. It was almost certainly New York – in the distance, I thought I could make out what looked like the Hudson River, with New Jersey beyond it – though there were none of the other familiar landmarks I associated with the city.

I brought my attention back to the woman behind the desk. She eyed me evenly, a tight, close-lipped smile locked into position on her unblemished face. There was something reptilian about her; at any moment I expected her tongue to come lashing out to snare the fly that was buzzing noisily around one of the windows, searching for an exit. "Thank you, Mr. Block," she said. "Please wait downstairs in the lobby. We'll call for you when we've made a decision."

I thanked her and stood up to leave, my mind racing to piece together what was happening. There had been some sort of interview. That much I could guess from what the woman had said. No sooner had the realization come to me than snippets of memory began surfacing through the fog. The interview had gone well. Surprisingly well, upon reflection. There had been none of the probing questions, the challenges to my veracity that I would have expected from a legitimate inquiry. Perhaps they were only observing form, I considered, going through the motions to give the appearance of due process. It had all been too easy, too polite.

Leaving the office, I shuffled down a long corridor, its plain white walls and matching floor rendered all the more stark by the fluorescent lamps overhead. The light made it hard to focus. Everything took on the soft, hazy appearance of a fever dream. My footfalls echoed off the tile before vanishing down the hallway's great expanse. I had never felt so small.

An elevator carried me down and deposited me into a cavernous, marble lobby. On the walls hung portraits of various men in dark suits who wore on their faces the cold sneer of officialdom. One day these might be my bosses, I thought, an idea that seemed at once hopeful and tragic.

Stepping outside for some fresh air, I winced at the bitter cold. A layer of soot-colored snow covered much of the sidewalk, the remnants of a winter storm that must have passed through the city days ago. I looked up and down the block. On one corner, above a concrete staircase that plunged down below street level, was a sign that read "Plymouth Station", beneath which was the image of a winged skull. I was struck by an eerie sense of familiarity, as if looking upon a childhood home I had not seen for years.

The wind was picking up. It perforated my jacket, the cold pricking my skin like a swarm of wasps. I retreated back to the lobby. As I entered, the receptionist at the front desk beckoned me over and handed me a telephone receiver. "Hello?" I said, as I placed it to my ear.

The voice of the woman who had interviewed me came through the earpiece. "I'm sorry I can't bring you back up to make you an offer in person, but we're extremely busy right now," she said.

"Does that mean I'm hired?"

"That's right. All you have to do is accept."

"What exactly is the job title?"

"You'll be a level-one Scraper. That's *entry* level."

"A Scraper?"

"Don't wear anything fancy," she said. "We'll give you a uniform to change into."

The 'uniform' in question turned out to be a full-body hazmat suit. It was the morning of the following day. I was in front of a squat, warehouse-like building that I took to be a Department of Public Works depot of some sort. My new supervisor, Chuck – a weary-looking but friendly man who resembled a walrus – welcomed me and a handful of other new recruits, then demonstrated the finer points of putting on the suit and making sure it was sealed correctly. "Is all this really necessary?" I said, as I tested my breathing apparatus.

Chuck grunted. "Those bodies get pretty rank. You don't want to be breathing that in. Not to mention the radiation."

Once we were suited up, we clambered into the back of a van and started off, turning onto Broadway and heading downtown toward Canal Street. The farther south we went the thinner the crowd on the sidewalks became, until it began to seem as if the whole city had been deserted. Rubble littered the streets. Buildings that had been partially or totally destroyed left gaping holes in the skyline, growing more frequent with every block.

"That's why they sent us to clean up," said Chuck, noticing me staring out the window. "It's getting so bad even the parts merchants can't stand to come down here, let alone the regular folk. Some people still have jobs down here, you know."

"What's a parts merchant?" I said.

"You'll see 'em. They used to be everywhere, hundreds of 'em, like swarms of flies. Now there are probably less than a dozen on even the busiest days. The ones who still bother to show up hang around the Financial District waiting for fresh jumpers. Can you imagine, surviving a cataclysm like that and then taking your own life?" He shook his head. "Anyway, when the parts merchants find a body, they take all the usable stuff – eyes, kidneys, limbs – anything that didn't get crushed by the fall. Then they sell 'em to hospitals or direct to consumer."

"Is that legal?"

Chuck shrugged. "Beats me. If it ain't, no one's doing anything about it. We're the only officials who come down this way, and we ain't arresting nobody. All we do is clean up the bodies. That's it. 'Just get rid of the bodies', the bosses say. As far as I'm concerned, the merchants are doing us a favor."

We kept driving, past Trinity Church, then left onto Exchange Place. "Now," said Chuck, "you'll really see something." The van pulled over and everyone clambered out of the back. No sooner had I jumped down to the pavement than I froze. On the sidewalk below the Stock Exchange was a mountain of bodies reaching at least thirty feet into the air.

"They don't all jump on that spot," said Chuck. "That wouldn't work anyway - as you can see the pile's almost up to the third-story windows now. We made this ourselves." He went back to the van and took out a wide, steel-framed object that resembled a cow catcher from the front of a train. "This is your main tool. You just get back here behind it, see, and grab these two handles. There are wheels on either side, so it moves real easy. Then you just walk up and down the pavement, collecting any bodies that might be in your way. Try to push ‘em over in this direction, into the pile.”

“What do we do with the pile?” asked one of the other new guys.

“Depends,” said Chuck. “We used to take all the bodies we found south of Wall Street and push ‘em straight through Battery Park into the harbor. But there got to be so many of ‘em the ferries couldn’t get through to Staten Island. Plus it was attracting schools of sharks. So, the city started loading ‘em onto barges and dumping ‘em in Fresh Kills. Only the city’s broke now, and there’s no more room in the landfill. They tried burning ‘em, but the smell was unbearable. So for now we’re just piling ‘em up and waiting for orders.”

Chuck gave everyone their assignment. Mine was the small section of Pine Street between Water and Pearl, something easy to get my feet wet. I grabbed my scraper and work kit – which included, amongst other things, a shovel, a bone saw, a propane torch and a bottle of bleach – and started off. On the corner of the small alley connecting Exchange Place and Wall Street, I passed two men in nylon track suits crouched over a dead body. Beside them on the ground were surgical kits. The men were busy making incisions in the right side of the dead man’s stomach. They glanced at me without expression as I passed, the skin on their faces and necks mangled by burn scars.

When I reached the edge of my sector, I got down to work. The scraper glided along without so much as a bump, as if the pavement were a sheet of ice. Even with the first body I picked up and the stray trash that accumulated the scraper never lost momentum, never became heavy or burdensome. It felt right somehow, as if this job were my calling, though I rebelled at the idea the moment it was conceived.

I scraped three bodies the first day. When my route was complete I returned to the Stock Exchange, where the rest of the workers were putting away their equipment and winding down. Chuck was pleased with my performance. He told me to add my bodies to the edge of the pile. "If you see anything you want to take home, just toss 'em in one of those bags over there." He pointed to a pile of body bags next to the van.

"Take home?" I said.

"For fuel." Chuck waved off my protestations. "I know, I know. I just got done saying that the smell was unbearable. But that's burning them all at once, out here in the open. Now, I got me a good wood stove, excellent ventilation, and I gotta tell you it's saved me a fortune in heating costs. You know they're shutting off the power within the month, right?"

I shook my head.

"It's true," said Chuck. "Can't afford to keep the gas flowing. The Seneschal blames saboteurs in the Public Works Department. I think it's BS myself, but they're threatening to do an investigation, drag any suspected malefactors out to Utah for 're-education'. Not something I want any part of. Anyway, this kind of thing's gonna be a necessity soon, so you may as well get a jump on it. Now, here's some advice – those fat-cat CEO types might burn up real nice and bright and make people 'ooh' and 'ah', but for my money it's the junior executives you want to keep you warm through the winter. The narcissists, the gym rats. They won't light up the sky, but they're compact and lean and they'll give you a long, slow burn."

We talked through the afternoon. Soon it was four-thirty, quitting time. The sun was already setting, bathing Lower Manhattan blood-red. Past the Battery, the light glinted off the water as it roiled and crackled like some sweeping fire that would one day engulf the entire city. Behind me, I could hear the scuttling of rodents' feet; the pile of bodies swayed and lurched like a drunk trying to keep his balance as he clawed his way home.

Chapter 5

When I woke up my face was on fire. A dry, racking cough sent me into convulsions; my chest felt like the heavy bag at Joe Frazier's the day after the champ found out that his girl had been cheating on him. Instinctively, I reached out and gripped the couch to keep from falling. Light streamed in through the windows and bullied its way past my eyelids, as abrasive as tear gas. I squinted and shielded my face with a hand as I tried to orient myself. Once my vision adjusted, I saw that I was back in my apartment. The TV was still on, though the news had been replaced by a rerun of some cop show from the 1980s. Something damp pressed against my arm – a puddle of drool, soaked into the cushions. The burning I had felt was the sun, much lower in the sky now and shining through a chink in the living room blinds onto the exact spot where I had been resting. With a start I saw that it was already seven o'clock, only an hour until I was supposed to meet BB.

I stumbled to the shower, washed and shaved, and put on a fresh pair of clothes. By the time I was groomed and fully conscious again it was a quarter to eight. I grabbed my gym bag and headed out, pausing at the door to give one last look around the apartment. For the first time since moving in I considered the place I had called home for the past four years. Its drab, cookie-cutter design and general air of neglect stirred within me no feelings of nostalgia. There was no art on the walls, no pictures of family or friends, nothing that would give an observer any insight into the person who lived there. Nevertheless, there was a finality to stepping outside and locking the door behind me that I hadn't reckoned with. For the first time it began to sink in that I would not be coming back, not ever.

Two female voices nearby startled me. I slammed the door shut, as if there were something incriminating inside I didn't want anyone to see. Glancing over my shoulder, I watched the owners of the voices – residents of the neighboring building – pass by, conversing amongst themselves and seemingly unaware of my presence. Turning back to the door, I tested the handle and confirmed it was locked. As a final act, to prevent my all-too reliable cowardice from dissuading me from carrying out my mission, I had left my only set of keys on the kitchen counter. There was no turning back – that's what I kept telling myself, at least, as if a locked apartment door were as inexorable as the passage of time. Periodically, during one of my increasingly rare moments of lucidity, I've heard myself mutter out loud, seemingly apropos of nothing, "I could have called a locksmith." But those who hear me pay little mind.

They tell me I say much stranger things on a regular basis.

I turned and scurried across campus, doing everything possible to make the act of walking to a gymnasium with a workout bag look as suspicious as possible. Rather than holding the straps in one hand and walking at a normal pace, I clutched the bag to my chest and cast furtive glances left and right, looking for all the world like a rat defending a hard-won piece of cheese.

Campus was largely empty and oddly still. Many students had already gone home for break or were out celebrating, while those unfortunates who still had finals ahead of them were sequestered in their rooms or the library studying. Consequently, my lunatic scuttling went unobserved until finally I reached the front door of the athletic center and slipped inside. From the entranceway I could hear muffled shouting and the arrhythmic thumping of a dozen basketballs inside the gym. I tried one of the doors. Finding it unlocked, I eased it open a few inches and peered in through the crack.

In contrast to the peacefulness outside, the gym was a hive of activity. Dozens of young men were playing in one of two pickup games that were taking place simultaneously on the side baskets. I scanned the players on the court, then the ones along the sidelines or in the bleachers waiting to take the next game. No sign of BB. Slipping the door shut again, I turned down the adjoining corridor and circled around to the back of the gym, then down the stairs that led to the locker room. I found it deserted, save for the odd pair of shoes or a shirt or bag that had been discarded beneath one of the benches. Picking out an empty locker, I opened my bag and began to change.

Although I've always been in fair shape, I lack the dexterity and coordination of a natural athlete. I was not the type to seek out pickup games to fill my free time. Whereas sports bring out in others a competitive spirit that pushes them to realize their best selves, in me it produces a profound anxiety that I will never measure up to those around me. That anxiety began rearing its head as I slid off my jeans and put on my only pair of shorts, a faded pair of Umbros that constituted the entire legacy of my tenure with the junior varsity soccer team in high school. "It doesn't matter how well you play," I thought to myself. "This is all just a cover."

Or at least I believed they had been my thoughts; to my surprise, they continued of their own volition. "If you're still nervous just focus on what you're good at. Run hard, play good defense, and if you end up with the ball pass it to someone else."

I turned around. BB was standing behind me, a Cheshire grin on his face. "Didn't think I'd make it, did you?" he said. Untrue, I responded. I had never doubted him for a minute. BB sat down beside me and put his hand on my shoulder. "That means a lot," he said. "We're going to need that, you know – trust – with what we're about to do." He opened his own bag and began changing. It was all I could do to keep from gawking. BB wore a sleeveless t-shirt, or rather a t-shirt that had once had sleeves but had had them ripped off. Frayed threads still dangled from the rims of the armholes, which distracted only somewhat from the dark smudges and streaks that covered the chest and back area. This he tucked into denim shorts, the waistband cinched tight with a brown vinyl belt. On his head he wore a black-and-white zebra print bandana, and on his feet, checkered boat shoes paired with ankle socks. It was the most ludicrous basketball uniform I had ever seen, and yet, not a single person looked at us or made a comment as we walked onto the court and took our places along the sidelines. A few other unattached players who had been milling around gravitated in our direction. Soon we had assembled a team and gotten ourselves onto the waiting list.

Eventually our turn came, and I'm relieved to say that I acquitted myself reasonably well. The same couldn't be said for BB. Not five minutes into the game, BB had out-leapt one of the opposing players to snag an errant jump shot. After coming down with the ball, he held it above his head, arms akimbo, and swung wildly with his elbows, catching one of the opposing players across his jaw. The other man flailed backwards, blood-flecked saliva spraying from his mouth and spattering across the hardwood floor. The man's teammates rushed forward, fists clenched, but several neutral observers ran onto the court and got in the middle, preventing what could have been a brawl.

"All right!" shouted one of the neutrals, as the shoving continued. He was a giant of a man, all rippling muscles and standing at least a head taller than anyone else on the court. Even those whose passions were running hottest lost their nerve the moment he spoke up. "Cool it! It's basketball, it happens," he said, shooting BB and me a warning look even as he formed a protective wall in front of us. "He all right?" he said, gesturing toward the guy BB had hit, who was sitting up now holding his jaw. A teammate sitting near him said a tooth had been knocked loose, but that he was ok. "Good," said the giant. "You," he said to BB, "apologize to him." BB held up his hands as if to say "no argument", then walked over to where the other man sat, held out his hand and said he was sorry. For good measure, I followed suit. Things seemed to diffuse from there. Some grumbling could be heard as the giant tossed the ball back to us and strode off the court, and some angry looks were directed our way – as many toward me, it seemed, as toward BB. Guilty by association, I supposed. As the teams separated, I leaned over and mumbled into BB's ear, "Are you nuts?" He smirked. "This game is our alibi," he said. "I'm just making sure everyone remembers us."

The gym closed at midnight. BB and I continued playing off and on until a quarter to twelve, at which time we said goodbye to our teammates and the other players that had stuck around to the end. Then we left and descended again to the locker room to get our bags.

"Should we get changed?" I said.

BB shook his head. "No showers, no changing. Think about it. If we were really here just to play basketball all night, would we bother showering or putting on a new set of clothes? No, we'd just head back to our apartments and clean up there before bed." He inspected his bag one last time before swinging it up onto his shoulder. "Not to mention," he continued, "taking down that statue could be hard work. Nerve-racking too. Say we get interrupted in the middle of the job. We manage to hide our tools and the truck's not in position yet, but we're covered in sweat and we both have bags packed. Well, now we have an excuse – we just came from the gym. In fact, make sure we pass through one last time before we leave. Pretend we forgot something. Everyone will see us with our bags and that we haven't changed our clothes. They can vouch for us if anyone starts asking questions."

We did just that, saying a second goodnight to everyone before stepping out into the cool night air. Aside from the diminished sounds still coming from inside the gym there were no signs of life. BB began walking in the direction of the fountain while I scurried after him, eager to stay in his orbit. The deeper into the center of campus we moved the more isolated we became. The air had a staid, vacuum-like quality that seemed to smother the sounds of our footfalls. The lampposts lining the walkways were spread out at too-great intervals, and the bluish light they gave off served only to deepen the surrounding shadows.

We had already passed the outer ring of shrubbery and were nearly to the benches before I realized that we had reached our destination. "What now?" I said, but BB continued walking straight through the circle, past the fountain and out the opposite side, heading toward the other end of campus. "Time to get the truck," he said, without turning around.

Once more I scrambled after him, past the administrative buildings and across Main Street, then down a series of smaller side streets full of tightly packed subdivisions that served as student housing during the school year. Empty beer cans, bottles and other trash were strewn across the lawns, the detritus of the many parties that were taking place that evening. The stillness that had dominated the center of campus was gone, replaced by the pulsing thump of speakers blasting out music from behind the walls of what seemed like every house we passed.

We continued on, making several twists and turns until at last we came to a faded, seafoam-green Victorian house wedged in between two similarly styled neighbors, each separated by a narrow driveway. It was to the driveway of the seafoam house that BB led me, where the moving truck he had told me about was parked. Unfortunately, a dark-blue Mini Cooper was parked directly behind it. BB frowned at the car as he approached, leaning down close and squinting as if he were studying some rare species of insect. At last he straightened and turned toward me. "This wasn't here when I parked the truck."

I frowned. "You don't say."

BB checked his watch. "Twelve-twenty. Soames will have just passed the fountain." As if that settled the matter he squeezed through the space between the Mini Cooper and the house and circled around to the driver's side of the truck. "Get in."

"What are you doing?" I said, moving to obey his command even as I asked the question. There was barely room for a person to squeeze past the car, let alone another vehicle. The houses on either side formed a sort of tunnel that boxed us in, making it impossible to sneak the truck out through the front lawn. Although there was some empty space ahead of us, it quickly terminated in a garage and large wooden fence that formed a barrier across the back of the property.

I clambered into the passenger's seat, wincing at the metallic echo the door made when I slammed it shut. BB pulled a key from his jacket pocket, put it in the ignition and turned. The engine sputtered for a moment before roaring to life like some angry beast that had been awakened too early from its slumber.

"Where are we going?" I said, looking in the sideview mirror to confirm that the Mini Cooper hadn't magically disappeared. Without answering, BB put his hand on the gear shift and pulled back. A shudder passed through the truck's frame. We began inching forward. Though the headlamps were not turned on there was enough light coming from the street to see the door of the garage approaching us at a steady clip. Less than ten feet away, BB showed no signs of slowing down. "BB, the garage!" I said, pointing through the windshield. He kept going. Five feet away. We were so close now I could see nothing but the door, filling our entire view and getting nearer by the second. "For Christ's sake, BB!" I shouted, wondering if he had gone mad. Just as I hunched back in my seat and braced for impact, the truck lurched to a halt. BB shifted into reverse and checked his mirror.

By the time it dawned on me what he intended to do it was too late to object. There was a 'thump' as his foot slammed down on the gas pedal. A banshee wail split the air as the truck's tires spun against the asphalt. We rocketed backwards, the garage receding in front of us as if we were watching a film strip being played in reverse. There was a deafening roar of twisted metal and broken glass as the truck's cargo box smashed into the Mini Cooper. Bright orange sparks arced from the pavement and rained down around us like a firework display as we bulldozed the tiny car across the street and up over the curb on the opposite side.

Free of the driveway now, the truck sat sputtering in the center of the street. My hand gripped the armrest as I gasped for air, certain now that we were doomed. There couldn't have been a soul within a mile radius that hadn't heard the collision. "Jesus Christ, do you know what you've done?" I said, but BB showed no such compunction. He wrenched the steering wheel to the right, shifted into drive and sped away toward campus.

We drove in silence for the first few blocks. BB tapped his hand against the top of the steering wheel, beating out an awkward rhythm. Though he tried to act casual I could see the lines of concern creasing his face. His breathing was shallow and quick. We weaved through the back streets. Another turn and we could see Main Street at the end of the block. Beyond it was campus. Every impulse told me to open the door and jump out, to walk away and pretend none of this had ever happened.

"Sorry I had to do that," said BB, his voice measured.

"Had to?!" I turned to glare at him. "You didn't *have* to do anything!"

"I did," said BB. "Look." He pointed to the dashboard clock. "It's already twelve-thirty."

"So?"

"Soames passed by the fountain fifteen minutes ago."

"So wait until he makes his next round. Or do it tomorrow, what's the difference?"

BB didn't answer. When we reached the intersection with Main Street he turned right and drove slowly along the edge of campus, scanning the view outside his window for something. "The police will be looking for us," I said. "The second someone sees what happened back there we're finished."

"No one saw us," said BB. "Did you see anyone on the street?"

"The noise alone…!"

BB waved his hand, dismissively. "It's a party night. You heard all the music. No one heard us, I promise."

"BB…" I shifted in my seat to face him. "At some point, someone is going to see that car smashed to bits on the neighbor's lawn. When that happens, we are screwed. It doesn't take a genius to figure out that there was a moving truck parked in front of the car that's now missing. The only way this truck could have gotten out of the driveway was to move that car out of the way. How many moving trucks fitting this description do you think there are within five miles of here? Hell, within fifty miles?"

He nodded, appearing to chew over what I'd said. Being the logical choice, I assumed he would abandon his plan and the truck and try to figure out the quickest way out of town. Instead, he said, "We're going to have to work fast." There were no cross streets on either side of us. Nevertheless, BB wrenched the wheel hard to the left, bouncing the truck up over a curb ramp that led onto one of the paved walkways traversing the school grounds. We followed its snaking path past rows of azalea bushes and around the Science and Technology building, the pavement so narrow that only one side of the truck's tires was able to drive on it at any given time.

BB doused the headlights, and the world descended into darkness. Objects seemed to appear in front of us like magic – park benches, hedges, trees. Only the lampposts gave themselves away. “Slow down!” I hissed, as we grazed a garbage can, but BB said there was no time. The ‘bang’ it made as it tipped over onto the sidewalk sounded like TNT to my ears. I crouched low in my seat, as if somehow the thousands of people I imagined were watching us would somehow overlook me if I were only a few inches shorter. Another lamppost passed, and suddenly we were plunged into an even deeper darkness than before. Everything past the windshield was black, as if we’d taken a wrong turn and driven off the end of the Earth.

“Almost there…” breathed BB, steadying himself as he lifted one hand from the wheel and gestured out into the nothingness in front of us. I was certain he’d gone crazy or was messing with me, but then I noticed it far off in the distance. A tiny pinprick of light, like a lone star in an otherwise devoid universe. Then I remembered the notes BB had showed me.

“That’s it,” I said. “The fountain.”

BB nodded. He hadn’t exaggerated. It was harder to notice in the daytime, but at night the fountain’s isolation from the rest of campus became apparent. What light there was coming from the lamps behind the benches was mostly smothered by the trees and flower bushes that ringed the area on all sides. The lawn separating the fountain from the nearest buildings stretched a quarter mile or more in every direction. The truck bounced and shook as we rambled across the grass, and yet the fountain never seemed to get closer; it hung there in the distance, tantalizing us like some desert watering hole we'd hallucinated. It felt as though we would never quite make it, but soon enough the truck began slowing, until finally we stopped beside a copse of maple trees just a few hundred feet from our destination.

"Take the wheel," said BB, rolling down his window before opening the door to hop out. I looked out the window to see if anyone might be watching, but the maple trees formed a barrier that shielded us from view. "Drive slow," said BB, from down on the lawn. "I'll walk alongside and direct you."

The directions BB shouted to me - "A little to your left!...Now straighten out!...Careful, there's a ditch coming!... Slower…Ease in…" – didn't seem to correspond whatsoever to the topography outside. I blindly followed his lead, the landscape nearly as shrouded in darkness as it had been out on the quad. Soon a milky, blue light pushed through the branches, growing brighter as we circled past the last of the maples. Then we saw him standing above the lapping water, glinting silver in the moonlight like some favored son of Selene – Thomas Bartholomew Bradford. At BB's signal I stopped the truck, put it in park and hopped down to stand beside him. We walked over to edge of the fountain and looked up at Bradford, saying nothing. Night had not cowed him in the least. He peered out over us into the blackness with the same cold command, as if infinite nothingness were just one more foreign land to conquer.

BB hopped back in the truck and turned it around so the cargo door was pointed toward the fountain. He barreled backwards, spraying grass and dirt everywhere, looking for all the world like he intended to ram his rear bumper straight through Bradford's bronze kneecaps. Bradford did not flinch, of course, and BB – upon reaching the edge of the fountain – slowed down and eased the back tires up the side and onto the top of its marble retaining wall. The truck came to rest at an angle, its back end raised in the air like some wild animal in heat. Bradford sneered his approval.

"Get the tools," said BB, jerking his thumb toward the back of the truck as he got out. I circled around and hopped up onto the fountain's ledge. The marble was wet and slick as ice. I inched forward, sliding my feet bit by bit until I reached the cargo door, then clambered up onto the bumper and slid the door open. Inside was a canvas bag. It flopped and clanked in protest as I dragged it across the floor, my muscles straining with the exertion. It was so heavy that when I tossed it to BB the momentum almost sent both of us tumbling into the water. BB dropped the bag at his feet and rummaged around inside, producing at last a handheld rotary tool. He pressed a button on the tool's side and its blade whirred to life, emitting a high-pitched, demonic whine like some sadistic dentist's drill.

"Let's do this," he said. He hopped onto the ledge with me and promptly skidded across it and off the other side, feet spinning uselessly beneath him like a vaudevillian comic performing a slapstick routine. To his credit, he managed to toss the saw back onto dry land before falling flat on his back into the water. "Shit!" he cried, sending miniature tidal waves crashing in every direction as he leapt to his feet. "It's freezing in here!" Like a rhesus monkey, he sprang up onto the central pillar and clung to the statue with both hands. Once secure, he asked me to toss him the rotary tool. "Be careful not to cut yourself," I said as I threw it. BB found this funny for some reason and started chuckling. He lost his balance momentarily and reached out again with both hands to cling to the statue. Meanwhile, my throw was off-target. The tool went sailing past BB's shoulder and landed with a 'kerplunk' in the water. And that was the end of our only motorized saw.

"Shit!" we both said.

Our only remaining option was the hacksaw. This time I waded into the water and delivered it to

BB by hand. “Stay here,” he said. “We’ll have to take turns.” He lined the blade up with the head of one of the bolts and started sawing away, arm pumping back and forth like a piston on a steam engine. The sound it produced was unmistakably like that of something being sawed, but fifteen minutes later, clutching his triceps in pain, BB had only managed to make it about a third of the way through the first bolt. “Your turn,” he panted, beads of sweat replacing the fountain water that had begun to dry from his face.

I sloshed over into position, took up the saw and picked up where BB had left off. My admiration for him grew; after only a minute the muscles in my arm begged for mercy, and my pace began to slow. What sort of men were we, I wondered, this soft modern breed? Did the colonists who tamed this subarctic wilderness all those centuries ago, constructing in its place a seat of learning and culture with nothing but a few rudimentary tools and their bare hands, feel pain like this? Did their bodies scream for mercy after only two minutes’ work? Thomas Bartholomew Bradford would have had us flogged.

My self-flagellation was proceeding unabated when suddenly there was a ‘ping’, and a tiny piece of metal shot from the edge of my saw, skipped between Bradford’s legs and plunked down into the water. A now headless bolt remained where my blade had been cutting. We looked at each other, BB and I, awash in the glow of our first small success. With renewed energy we dove headlong into our task, the aches and pains of just a few minutes earlier dissipating as the finish line came into view. Trading off every few minutes, we had soon decapitated a second, and then a third bolt. When the fourth and final bolt was cut, we were so elated we embraced, BB letting loose an exultant whoop into the night air. But our joy was short-lived when we attempted to push the statue over and found it as intractable as ever.

BB, half perched on the pedestal and half in the water, hunched over and drove his shoulder into the statue like a linebacker hitting the practice sleds. With a grunt he went limp and slid panting into the pool. “It’s no use,” he said. “We took the nuts off, but the bolts are still intact.”

“Maybe we should get out of here,” I said.

BB ignored me and dragged himself out of the fountain, flopping onto the pavement like a beached fish. He stood up and peered into the distance. Bathed as we were in lamplight, the darkness outside of our circle was impenetrable.

Before I knew what was happening he had taken off running, swallowed up by the night as if he’d passed through a portal into another dimension. I called after him as loudly as I dared, but after a few tries it was clear he was out of earshot. I left the water myself and milled around beside the fountain, wondering if BB had abandoned me and calculating how long I was willing to wait before I started looking for ways to save my own skin.

Several minutes passed. Every time I set a deadline for myself, swearing that I would leave if he did not reappear by a certain time, I watched it elapse and then promptly set a new one. On one occasion I managed to leave the fountain altogether and walk as far as the line of maple trees we had first parked beside, but an approaching sound stopped me short. It was something much louder than a person's footsteps. As it got closer, I could make out the distinctive hum of a car's engine, not passing by on the road at the periphery of campus but coming toward me across the grass.

My first thought was that it was the police, and my knees buckled. But there were no flashing lights, no sirens. Perhaps they were being stealthy, I thought, afraid to alert me to their presence until there was no chance of my escape. As the noise got closer, however, it sounded too deep and growly to be a police car's engine. I searched for headlights but couldn't see any. By the time the pickup truck that was barreling toward me came into focus I barely had time to leap out of the way.

"Sorry!" yelled BB out the driver's window, grinning ear to ear as he went flying past me. I ran after him and arrived back at the fountain right as he was turning the pickup around to back it up toward the statue, just as he had done with the moving truck. It was an enormous machine, jacked high up off the ground on oversized tires like some hobbyist's monster truck. As its rear wheels climbed up onto the lip of the fountain, the truck's bed – a monstrous, swimming-pool sized thing – made contact with the statue, the bumper pressing itself into the small of Thomas Bartholomew Bradford's back. There was a sound like a spring uncoiling, then a pop, and over Bradford went like a toppled dictator. His head and shoulders landed inside the back of the moving truck and the momentum carried the rest of him forward, like a child diving headfirst down a sliding board. There was a resounding metallic 'gong' as the top of Bradford's skull impacted against the back of the cab.

Startled, I froze, as if the sound were a signal in a children's game to stop moving. BB stopped moving as well. With the statue dislodged the bed of the pickup was now suspended on the marble base where the statue used to be, its back tires half in the water and spinning uselessly, sending a fine mist up into the air.

Cautiously, BB climbed down from the pickup. Together we crept toward the moving truck, each step slow and deliberate as if we were approaching a wild animal we weren't sure was dead or alive. Logic told me to hop inside and drive away as fast as we could, but some primal instinct kept me glued in place. When we reached the back of the truck we stood on our tiptoes and peered inside. There was Bradford, face down on the floor as if passed out drunk, looking no worse for wear despite the impact. BB climbed up on the bumper and slipped inside, kneeling down to inspect the statue more closely. All of a sudden he began to laugh, a full-throated cackle that made him double over on the floor.

"What?" I said. He motioned for me to come inside. I did, and BB pointed toward Bradford's face.

"The nose!" he said, between fits. "Look at it!"

I crouched down to examine the statue's face. Bradford's nose was bent upward, the tip pointing toward his forehead and his nostrils flared, looking for all the world like an eight-foot-tall pig. Now I started laughing, rocking back and forth with my face in my hands, which started BB howling all over again. Whatever spell we had been under was broken. Our spirits soared. It felt like this were all just a senior prank we would commiserate about over beers when we were older.

As soon as we had collected ourselves, we climbed down, shut the back door and went right to the cab. BB had just started the engine and was about to pull out when a movement in the distance caught my eye. At first, I thought I was imagining things.

Whatever it was seemed to disappear the moment I tried to focus on it, an ephemeral thing flickering and swirling at the edges of my vision like eye flashes. Mentally, I replayed the events of that evening, trying to remember if I had hit my head at some point. BB gave no indication that anything was amiss. I blinked several times and squinted into the darkness. The flickering and swirling began to coalesce; there was a definite form to it now. As urgently as I could without making a scene, I reached over and tugged at BB's sleeve.

"What?" he said. I motioned for him to be quiet and pointed through the windshield at the shape approaching out of the blackness. BB followed the direction of my finger, and I heard his breath catch. "What the hell is that?" he said. Having no idea, I didn't bother to respond. Hurriedly, we rolled up the windows and sat, bodies rigid, watching in silence as the spectral figure floated toward us out of the gloom.

Or rather, doddered. As it came close enough to enter the fringes of the light being cast by the lamps behind us, we could see that the figure was Soames, as wizened and sunken as last year's jack-o'-lantern. He shuffled up the footpath, presumably on one of his rounds. Glancing down at the dashboard clock, I saw that it was 2:45am.

"Right on time," I said.

Soames hobbled forward past the front of the truck, until he was standing just outside my door. My mind raced to concoct a believable cover story as I reached over to roll down the window, but before I could even grasp the handle, I watched the top of Soames' head – a shock of bone-white hair as coarse as a hillbilly's table manners – bob past without the slightest hesitation and continue on through the courtyard.

BB and I looked at one another, then up to watch Soames' receding refection in the rearview mirror. "Do you think he saw us?" I said. BB shrugged. We waited until Soames had circled the fountain and disappeared down a different footpath. Finally, after another minute or so had elapsed, BB shifted the truck into drive and pressed down lightly on the accelerator. The truck shimmied and lurched forward in uneven, jerking movements, strained by the added weight in the back. Eventually we gained momentum and rolled out under cover of darkness, keeping our headlights turned off and retracing our route until we reached the edge of campus.

Pulling back onto Main Street, the mood grew tenser. While BB drove, I kept lookout for the police, but the coast proved to be clear. In the distance I thought I spotted flashing lights coming from the direction of the house where we had rammed the Mini Cooper. Perhaps all three of the town's patrol cars were too busy responding to the scene to come looking for us. Regardless, we slipped through downtown unnoticed and kept on driving, watching the houses thin out as we approached the outskirts of town and disappeared into the countryside.

The night seemed darker than was possible in the civilized world. No doubt someone raised in Big Sky country – where you can drive for a hundred miles without seeing a single building, and the night sky is so unsullied by artificial light that every star to the furthest ends of the Milky Way is visible – would find nothing unusual about it. But for those of us from the east coast, where each town blends into the next and even the most desolate highway is lined with streetlamps, rural New England after sunset is a shock to the senses. Driving along the backroads of New Hampshire and Vermont, we felt as if we had been transported to another century; I would not have been surprised to glimpse a horse-drawn carriage trotting past us in the other direction. The beams from our headlights seemed weak and ineffectual, as if the dark were pushing back against them.

When we reached upstate New York hours later, BB abandoned the backroads and merged onto the interstate, aiming us due south. "Is that a good idea?" I said, but BB was confident. "If there's one place a moving truck won't attract notice, it's New York City."

The miles ticked off one after the other. The highway was dull, but at least we could see what was in front of us. “What’s next?” I said. “What’s the plan?”

“No plan, remember?” said BB. “We just go where the journey takes us.”

“Where is it taking us?”

“Right now, toward New York,” he said. “After that, we do what adventurous Americans have always done – we head west.”

Chapter 6

The sky had brightened so gradually that I barely realized it was morning. I gazed half-lidded out the window at Newark, splayed out beneath the highway like an unconscious drunk. We had just passed New York, that towering monument to wealth our forefathers had erected and aimed across the Atlantic to prove to the fuddy-duddies in Europe that the American Dream was real. Pressing on to the west, however, the scenery began to change. Overpasses crisscrossed and interlaced to no apparent purpose, arcing overtop of impound lots ringed with barbed-wire fences. Squat, brick warehouses the size of entire city blocks lined the banks of the Passaic River, around which tractor-trailers and shipping containers were scattered like some colossal child's discarded playthings. In the distance, half-filled office buildings sagged beneath the weight of their own pretensions. It was an angular, brutalist vista of concrete and steel, so uniformly bleak that even the small patches of nature that managed to poke through the cracks had an air of premature decay. I could go on, but why? It is not to damn Newark that I tell you this. It is only to tell you that it was upon reaching Newark that we were finally forced to leave the interstate.

"How long have we been driving?" I said, my voice hoarse, as if I'd just woken from a long nap.

“Five hours, give or take,” said BB, fiddling with the radio until he found a station that came in clearly. An announcer with a patrician accent was re-capping the local headlines during the top-of-the-hour news break. A man had been arrested by New Jersey State Police for killing a young girl and critically wounding the girl’s mother in Florida. The mother had refused to have sex with the suspect after the two had struck up a conversation at a grocery store in Kissimmee, after which the suspect had escorted the woman and her daughter back to their apartment. When his advances were rebuffed, the suspect had removed a handgun that had been concealed beneath his shirt and shot the woman through the head. He then tied the woman and her daughter together back-to-back, drove them to the Everglades in the trunk of the mother’s car and dumped them into the swamp for the gators to finish off. In an attempt to dispose of the car, the suspect drove north on I-95 straight through the night, snorting methamphetamine along the way to stay awake. When he reached Newark, the suspect finally pulled off the highway and stopped at the nearest body shop he could find, where he asked a man standing by the garage if he knew of, “a chop shop where they can make a car disappear”. The man in the garage turned out to be an off-duty State trooper who was having his own car serviced. He immediately placed the suspect under arrest and searched the woman's car, where he found traces of her blood inside the trunk. What's more, while the little girl did indeed die in the swamp, the mother somehow managed to survive the bullet wound and drag herself to the berm of the road, where a passing motorist saw her and called for help. She was taken to an area hospital and was in critical condition, but expected to survive. State prosecutors hoped she would recover enough to testify by the time the case went to trial.

"Next," said the announcer, "police in New Hampshire are seeking the public's help in foiling what appears to be a prank gone bad. Officials at Braithwaite College awoke this morning to find a bronze statue of Thomas Bartholomew Bradford, a 17th-century benefactor who helped found the school, missing from its pedestal near the center of campus, where it had stood for more than a century…"

BB and I exchanged glances.

"Witnesses described seeing a white and orange rental truck driving away from the scene early this morning, around the time the statue was assumed to have been taken. Police in surrounding states, including New York and New Jersey, have been provided a description and are actively involved in the pursuit."

"Take the next exit," I said.

We veered off the highway and descended into an industrial area, settling onto a road lined with shipping and storage depots that followed the river's edge. It had come to this, then – lumped in with meth-addled child murderers. The precariousness of our situation was all too apparent. Like a weak-bladdered motorist with no rest stops in sight, I searched frantically for a secluded spot off the side of the road, somewhere we could ditch the truck and slip away unnoticed. BB must have been thinking the same thing. "There," he said, pointing down the road toward a massive warehouse. The perimeter of the property was surrounded by a chain-link fence, but I could just make out a gap at the far end where a gate appeared to have been left open.

I shook my head. "If the gate's open people are there. We'll get caught."

"These places are huge," said BB. "And it's still early. There probably aren't that many people there yet. Let's take our chances. If anyone sees us, we'll tell them we got off the highway by mistake and got lost trying to turn around."

We turned in at the gate and crept along the side of the depot, weaving through stacks of crates and shipping pallets like a parent tiptoeing across the room of their sleeping toddler. The property seemed quiet, but it was clear we were not alone. Everywhere were little signs of life – lights blinking next to a loading dock, the distant whir of operating machinery, furtive movements glimpsed inside the building that may or may not have been imagined – that kept us on edge. The deeper we moved into the property, away from the road, the more trapped I felt. The veracity of our alibi diminished with every extra foot we drove, every second we neglected to turn the truck around and return to the highway.

Finally, toward the back of the warehouse, not far from the river, we spotted a fenced-in compound off the side of the main building, next to a wooded area. Inside it, shipping containers were stacked around the perimeter at varying heights like a giant bar graph. Only three sides of the compound were enclosed; the fourth remained open and allowed vehicles enough room to carry containers in and out. We turned in, snaking our way through the maze of crates and feeling some relief at the cover they provided. When we could no longer see the warehouse, BB stopped the truck and we got out to survey the situation.

"What now?" I said. "Should we just leave it and go?

"Hold on," said BB. He walked past a couple of the containers and yanked on their doors, but they refused to budge. Down the row he went, testing the containers one by one. After the first dozen turned out to be locked neither of us were prepared when the latch on the thirteenth container popped open without resistance. BB and I each grabbed a door and pulled them open, revealing the container's cavernous interior.

It was mostly empty, save for some shrink-wrapped pallets filled with what looked like books stacked in one of the corners. Lying on the floor in front of us was a forklift ramp. BB extended it down to the ground, then hopped back in the truck and eased it up the ramp. The container was just tall enough for the truck to fit inside. When he had pulled in as far as he could, he hopped out with our bags and ran around to the back, still clutching the keys in his hand. Kneeling down, he used one of the keys to unscrew the license plate and remove it from the bumper. When he had rejoined me on the ground, I closed the doors and held them while BB fastened the latch. On the door, inches from my face, the number 'XLJ 456427' was stenciled in white paint.

"What are you going to do with that?" I said, pointing at the license plate that was still in BB's hand.

"Get rid of it," he said. "But not here. The further away the better."

"They'll still figure out who the truck belongs to," I said. "There's the VIN number, first of all. Not to mention the statue in the back."

"Can't be too careful," he said. "Besides, even if they do figure out what truck this is, they won't get my name. I used a fake ID when I rented it."

"Yeah?" I said. "What name did you use?"

A flicker of something passed over BB's face, barely perceptible. He shrugged. "I don't remember," he said, sounding annoyed. "Look, we need to get out of here. Follow me."

We grabbed our bags and started off. BB led the way as we crouched low and slunk along the edge of the fence, tiptoeing like a pair of hapless burglars in an old silent comedy. I assumed we would backtrack toward the highway, but when we reached the entrance to the compound BB turned left instead, making a mad dash for the cover of the woods. I scrambled after him. We plunged through the undergrowth, elbowing aside branches and moving ever deeper until the warehouse was no longer visible behind us. Our pace slowed as we were forced to pick our way through a dense thicket of brambles, their thorns tearing at our clothes and skin no matter how carefully we tried to navigate them. After a short time, we could see the vegetation thinning out to our right and the Passaic's dark waters rolling past on their way to Newark Bay. Though the river's banks were bare we stuck to the cover of the trees until it was no longer possible.

The woods continued for another mile or so, then abruptly stopped, as if a massive machete had come down from the sky and cleared away everything past that point. Trees and wild grasses gave way to a manicured lawn at the outer edge of an industrial park. A cluster of boxy office buildings surrounded by a massive parking lot sat a few hundred feet to our left, forming a barrier between us and the road.

"I think we're ok," said BB. "No one will notice us here." He nodded toward the water. "Let's stick to the river as long as we can."

The sun was high and the air muggy by the time we reached downtown Newark. The sprawling industrial lots and relative quiet that had marked the beginning of our journey had been replaced by dense city housing and the roar of cars on the elevated highways above us. A minor league baseball stadium could be seen in the distance. I was looking for a sign to tell me the name of the team when BB tapped me on the shoulder and pointed to an onramp on our right, snaking upward toward the Essex Freeway.

"Great," I said. "Now find us a car."

"We'll hitch," said BB.

I started to protest, but BB had already veered off and was making a beeline for the connector road leading to the ramp. It was a busy two-lane road with no sidewalks or berm to speak of, but BB swung himself up over the guardrail anyway and plopped down on the edge of the outer lane, sticking out his thumb as cars whizzed past only inches away from him.

I hurried after him, yelling as I ran. "Are you crazy? Get out of there!"

"What for?" yelled BB, over the traffic noise.

"You're going to get killed!"

He waved me away with his left hand while continuing to thumb with his right. "I'll be fine!"

"I'm not hitching," I said. I had reached the guardrail now and stood across from BB. Even from where I was, I could feel the breeze from the passing cars tousling my hair. "Let's go."

"What do you mean let's go?"

"You heard the radio," I said. "What if the person who picks us up heard the same report? What if they put two and two together? It's not worth it. Let's just keep walking into town, find a bus station or something."

He shook his head. "I'm not wasting money on a bus."

"I'm going, BB."

He turned and looked at me, silent for a moment. As if coming to a decision, he shrugged and focused his attention back on the road. "Fair enough," he said. "This is where we part ways."

Apprehension seized me. I hadn't considered the possibility that we would split up so soon. The abruptness with which the moment had arrived gave me pause. For a moment I lingered there, trying to think of a way to convince BB he was making a mistake. But the traffic was growing heavier. Drivers hammered their horns or cursed out their windows, screaming at BB to get off the road. Too much attention was being drawn to us. "I'm sorry," I said, turning to leave.

"Don't be," said BB. "We make the choices we make." He lowered his thumb for a moment and leaned over the guardrail. "Go west," he said. "We'll see each other again, if it's meant to be." He winked, then leaned back into the road and stuck out his thumb.

"Later, BB," I said. No reply. I started walking away, looking back every so often as I waited for a response. But BB did not speak or look back at me. It was as if I were already a distant memory.

It took me another hour to locate the Greyhound station on Raymond Plaza. The woman at the ticket counter gave me the once over as I approached, barely trying to conceal her distaste. Only then did I become aware of how repulsive I must have seemed, my hair oily and reeking of dried sweat, my skin dotted with dozens of thorn scratches seeping blood.

"When's the next bus heading west?" I said.

She shrugged. “Lot of buses heading west.”

“The next one,” I repeated.

The woman wrinkled her nose, as if she smelled something sour. I made a mental note to brush my teeth as soon as I got the opportunity.

“Where are you trying to go?” she said.

“I…don’t know.” I stared open-mouthed at the floor as I mulled it over. The woman sighed in such a way that made clear she had spent too many years behind a counter talking to people like me. “California?” I said, at last.

“You ain’t sure?”

“California.”

“Ain’t no buses to California from here.” She narrowed her eyes at me, then turned and began typing something into her computer. “There’s a bus leaving in an hour that will take you to Salt Lake City. Lots of stops along the way, but you won’t need to transfer. Once you get to Salt Lake you can get a bus to Los Angeles or San Francisco or just about anywhere else you want to go.”

“Perfect,” I said. “How much?”

“Two twenty-five.”

“Two *hundred* twenty-five?”

“Dollars.”

“I don’t have that much.”

She arched an eyebrow. “You’re *kidding.*”

"Wait a minute." I rifled through my bag until I found my wallet. "Look, I've got…" I counted up my available cash. "One hundred sixty-five dollars!"

"Hmm…" She began typing again. "A hundred and fifty bucks will get you to Lincoln, Nebraska."

"Nebraska?"

"It's a state."

"And that's the furthest west you can get me?"

"No, that's the furthest west you can afford." She exhaled sharply, put her hands on the counter and leaned forward, eyes boring into mine. "Take it or leave it."

I took it. What else could I do? The universe had spoken.

Chapter 7

The bus carried us west, through Pennsylvania and into Ohio. The topography outside was like a dying man's heart monitor, its rhythms growing steadily fainter until flattening once and for all as we neared Indiana. I had never seen plains before. Staring at them now through the tinted lens of my bus window, their sheer magnitude struck me like a boxer's punch. It was as if God, in the middle of creating North America, had suddenly run out of things to express and had been content to just fill in the gap. They produced in me a paradoxical feeling of being isolated from the world, yet exposed, with nowhere to hide. A thoroughly paranoid feeling. All truth is paradox, I reflected. I wondered if I was starting to lose it.

Illinois was a checkerboard of brown and green stuck through with a million utility poles, like pins protruding from a gigantic cushion. People from Wisconsin call people from Illinois "flatlanders". People from Pennsylvania call people from Indiana "flatlanders", and people from Vermont call anyone whose family hasn't resided in Vermont for at least three generations "flatlanders", but from what I can tell the Wisconsinites got it right. Far off on the horizon I could see the earth's curvature and the ground falling away until all that remained was sky, a thing

I had only experienced once before when I had visited the sea as a child. It drove home the distance between BB and me. Wherever he was, it was unlikely I would see him again.

There is a palpable desperation aboard Greyhound buses. The very air smells of it, suffocating and sickly and redolent of unpleasant possibilities, like a hospital waiting room. The passengers exude none of the *joie de vivre,* none of the giddy anticipation that permeates every plane or train or ship I have ever ridden upon. No one rides a Greyhound because they want to. Every last person on that bus was compelled to be there by some unfortunate circumstance in their life. Those new passengers who boarded at each stop looked less road-weary perhaps, but every bit as sullen as the departing ones they replaced. The only difference was the length of time they had spent in our mobile purgatory.

One who had been there with me all the way from Newark was seated one row in front of me, across the aisle. He had the wavy, shoulder-length hair of a Seventies rock musician, with a scraggly, light-brown beard to match. The navy-blue tank top he wore showed off his stringy, muscular arms. There was a fidgety, impatient quality to him; when he wasn't shifting in his seat he was drumming his fingers on the armrests or thumbing through a book he kept lodged in the back of the seat in front of him, which he would shut and put away just seconds after opening. A sweaty film clung to his dark skin, despite the air conditioner running on high.

The cover of the man's book caught my eye. The title wasn't visible from where I sat, but the color scheme seemed familiar – white, with a blue bar running across the middle. Curious and more than a little bored from staring out the window, I craned my neck forward. "Excuse me," I said. At the sound of my voice the man leapt sideways and twisted in his seat as if he'd been jabbed with a cattle prod. His eyes bulged as I apologized for startling him. His mouth remained agape, as if an expression of shock had been permanently seared into his face. While I continued stammering how sorry I was to have disturbed him his eyes suddenly cleared, like a computer inside him had rebooted. "Who are you?" he grumbled, cutting me off.

I told him my name. The man looked me up and down, studying me. "Block?" he said. "Like a building block?"

"I suppose so," I said.

As if that settled something the man scooched toward me until his stomach was pressed against the armrest of his seat. He extended a hand across the aisle. I shook it, trying not to show my discomfort at its dampness or the stringent chemical smell that emanated from him.

"I'm Mortify," he said.

"Sorry?"

"My name," he said. "Mortify Goodfellow." If my confusion showed, it did not deter him. On the contrary, he seemed to grow more self-assured. His gaze was difficult to look away from. Tiny flames seemed to flicker and dance behind his eyes. "A good name is a thread tied about the finger, to make us mindful of the errand we came into the world to do for our master."

"Uh huh," I said. "I was just noticing the book you were reading…"

Mortify's face lit up. In a single motion he reached over and snatched the book out of its compartment, the way an animal might snatch a piece of food from the center of a snare. "You know the Word?" he said, holding it up for me to see. *Providence's Blessing*, it was called. No author was listed. Instead, it said it was "compiled by Fear-Gods Cromwell".

"No," I said. "That is, I haven't read it. Something about it seems familiar, though."

He nodded. "The first time I beheld the Word I felt the same way. The Truth always feels familiar." His gaze shifted to the middle distance and his voice began to quaver. "Of all histories of lives, I should think, the history of a man's own life must needs be most acceptable. To be able to read our lives from the womb to the present moment, from the cradle to the grave, would surely be a study as profitable as delightful." When he had finished, he met my eyes again. "You're not on your way to see the Seneschal, then?"

I shook my head, baffled.

"All the more meaningful that we should meet like this. A fellow traveler you are, if ever there was one." He handed the book to me, vibrating with excitement. "I'm on my way to the Temple right now for that very purpose - to learn to truly understand myself." As I reached out to take the book from him, he held it fast for a moment, hesitant to relinquish his grip. Finally, with a faint grin he patted the cover and released it into my hands. "Read," he said. "There are a lot of hours between here and Utah."

"My ticket's only good to Nebraska."

"Still…" He gestured to the book, then turned to face forward once more, pulling his knees up to his chest and hugging them so that he was curled into a ball. For the rest of the ride he stayed that way, not so much as glancing back at me. I could hear him muttering to himself, over and over, repeating some sort of mantra as he rocked back and forth.

Providence's Blessing looked like any other hardcover with a glossy dustjacket you might find in the Self-Help section of a chain bookstore. The cover design, the color palate, the less than sincere blurbs, even its length (289 pages, enough to look substantive without being intimidating). Between Mortify's obviously fabricated name, his spiritual-drifter attire and the book, I assumed he was headed to a retreat of some sort. Curious what could have been in store for me had I tagged along with him all the way to Utah, I opened to the prologue and began reading.

Providence's Blessing opens with something less than a stunner – "Fear-Gods" was not the author's (that is to say, the "compiler's", whatever that meant) given birth name:

> *"When I entered this world, my parents gave me a name. It was a perfectly suitable name for a perfectly secular world. I will not repeat it here. Know, however, that my rejection of it stems not from any animosity toward my mother and father; to the contrary, their sacrifice was my revelation. Many things, now they are revealed, seem very plain, as if we would have arrived at their certainty by time and reason alone. Do not be deceived. Every man would plead for the lawfulness of his chosen practice, as suited his fancy and agreed with his interest and appetites. He would call himself what please his Spirit, and not that which he is – a*

> *servant to our masters, and a vessel for their will.*
>
> *Some have asked me why I would deign to serve those whom I fear. There are times when fear is good. It must keep its watchful place at the heart's controls. I fear our Gods in that I hold them in awe and submit myself to them willingly. I fear our Gods in that I love them, just as I love this planet Earth that is our home, though it holds for us many terrors. By fearing the Gods, I fear nothing, for they remove all reason to fear."*

It sounded like garden-variety pablum you would hear in any Pentecostal church on a Sunday morning, except for his use of the word "Gods", in the plural. Intrigued, I continued reading, wondering if someone had found a way to marry polytheism with Christian mass-marketing techniques.

> *"Childhood is a myth slowly unravelling, a story that rewrites itself upon reflection every year that passes. I watched the seemingly idyllic marriage which brought me into this world disintegrate day by day. Without the wisdom to understand what was happening or the vocabulary to express my feelings, I could do nothing but sit idly by and*

watch my Eden engulf itself in flames. But now, with many years behind me, I realize that what I had regarded as a disintegration was in reality a stripping bare of artifice. Their marriage had been doomed from its inception, poisoned by a force no love can withstand – each of them wanted only those things from life which they could not have. Failing to achieve the impossible, they blamed each other.

When, at the age of twelve, I found my father hanging by his neck from the rafters in our garage it was my mother's words that struck me hardest of all – 'The spineless bastard!' she said. 'He didn't even have the guts to kill me himself! I have to do it, like everything else!' Even his suicide she viewed as an attempt to get one over on her, to claim some perceived moral high ground and punish her through shame and guilt. Sadly, she was probably right. In that moment, however, all this was unclear to me. I was too numb to do anything but stare. I did not even realize my mother had left the garage until I heard the 'bang' from inside the house. I ran to her bedroom to find her splayed across the floor, blood pouring from a hole in the top of her skull. Her final counterstroke. All of life reduced to a petty contest of wills inside a 1,400-square-foot house.

A small, black handgun – a .38, I know now, but just a gun to me then – lay on the carpet a few feet from my mother's hand. It was the first that I had learned our family even owned a gun. Its foreignness repulsed me. I yearned to be rid of it, to exorcise it from our house. The impulse was so strong that I went as far as to reach out toward the gun, thinking to grab it and run to the window to throw it outside. But as my hand got closer, a powerful sensation passed through me. Every muscle in my body contracted, and I fell to my knees. My limbs trembled. The world around me shifted in and out of focus. How much time passed or whether I lost consciousness I cannot say for certain. When the pressure finally subsided, I raised my head from the floor and found to my shock that I was not alone.

Two figures were in the room with me, standing at the foot of my parents' bed and looking down at where I lay. I use the word 'figures' deliberately; though humanoid in appearance, they were not human. Their heads were slightly too elongated, their facial features too piscine. An aura of silvery light surrounded them, undulating softly as if disturbed by a breeze I could not feel. Their heights differed – the figure on the left was as tall as a professional basketball player, his stature only exaggerated by the prostrate vantage point from which I beheld him. The figure on the right was much shorter, his head reaching only to his counterpart's shoulder. They gazed down at me, mute and expressionless. The light they gave off cast an obscuring shadow, as if they were each standing a few steps back through the doorway of a darkened room. This was my moment of revelation, my first contact with the Gods.

"Stand," said the taller one. I obeyed like a broken dog. "Why do you look so?" he said. "My parents are dead," I answered, gesturing to my mother as if perhaps they had not seen her lying there on the floor. "You grieve for them?" said the shorter one. I nodded, tears forming in my eyes. "Grieve not," he said. "Whatsoever comes to pass, the universe has ordained."

Seeing that his words had failed to pacify me, he beckoned me forward. Again, like a puppet guided by strings, I followed his command unquestioningly. The air grew progressively colder as I approached, until at last I could see my breath billowing in front of my face as I stood before them. "You blame yourself," said the taller one. "You believe that had you done something differently in your life somewhere along the way you would not have arrived at this low place you now find yourself. Know this, child, and may it be of some comfort to you – this could not have been avoided. Your belief otherwise belies your ignorance of the universe's perfection. Its purposes cannot be circumvented."

They each took a step apart then, and the taller one pointed to a spot on the wall between them. At first, I saw nothing. Then the silvery light they gave off began to swirl and writhe across the wall's surface, until at last in its center I could make out an image. A gleaming white palace stood on an otherwise barren plain. It was a classical Greek-style structure fronted by six towering Doric columns. Carved into the surface of its peaked roof was a relief depicting a line of strange-looking figures performing various activities. The ground itself was also white, sun baked and bleached of color. "Look closely at your destiny," said the shorter one.

I peered deeper into the image. A movement caught my eye. A tiny speck, looking no bigger than an ant, emerged from the columns and stepped out into the sunlight. As I watched it descend the stairs at the front of the building the image began to zoom in, like an aerial drone swooping down for a close-up. I could see it was a man, dressed all in black, which stood out starkly against the white background. He wore a loose-fitting shirt with wide sleeves that were gathered at the cuffs, knee-length pants, and a doublet overtop of a vest. A cape hung from his shoulders. On his head was a felt hat, turned up at the front and adorned with a buckle. This he removed before wiping his brow with the back of his hand. When his hand pulled away, a face that was strange and yet instantly familiar confronted me. It reminded me of my father in some intangible way. Only when the man reached up to touch his face, pressing the tips of his index and middle fingers against his eyebrow as he became lost in thought, did I realize I was looking at myself fully grown.

The moment this realization came to me, another spasm passed through my body. The room dissolved into white light, and I felt my arms and legs spread, splayed out as if I were falling through a bottomless void. When at last I awoke, several hours had passed. I was alone again, save for my mother's body. The blood had steadily drained from her, pooling around her head. She had a pale, waxy appearance. This time my emotions were steady. I bade her a silent goodbye, closed her eyes and then went to the phone to call 911. When the police and medics arrived, I was business-like, leading them through the house and recounting the timeline of events that had culminated in my parents' deaths. The lead detective on the case was unnerved by my demeanor. "He's in shock," I heard one of the medics say to him, when she thought I wasn't listening. "It's one of the brain's defense mechanisms. It will all hit him later. Right now, he's just dealing with the situation that's in front of him."

She was wrong, of course. This was not the mind closing off certain pathways to protect the body that houses it. To the contrary, my mind had been opened far beyond what the average person knows is possible. There was no need to ask why my parents had died, as so many people ask themselves in the aftermath of a tragedy. I already knew. Their deaths were written long ago, like everything else that happens in this world. My parents had to die to bring about my revelation, that I may know the Truth and share the Word with you so that you may be saved as well.

Accept the Truth. This is the core of my message. When it is raining, let it rain. Your rage is so much mist, dissipating in the light of the Word."

I had to hand it to Fear-Gods. In a saturated market of telling people how to think, act and believe, he had somehow managed to carve out a niche for himself. He was batshit crazy, of course. Maybe that's what his adherents found so compelling. "Authenticity", they probably called it.

I stopped reading as closely once the prologue ended and the book's focus shifted toward Fear-Gods' philosophy and teachings. It was familiar Prosperity Gospel stuff, exhorting his followers to strive, to reach out their thoughts and feelings to the universe so that it may deliver to them the success, riches and joy they desire. Of course, whether or not a person attains success, riches or joy has already been ordained by the Gods and nothing anyone says or does can change that. However, Fear-Gods posits, just as it was fated that the Truth would reveal itself to him, that he would write *Providence's Blessing* and that millions of people around the world would hear the Word, so too might it be preordained that those who hear the Word must accept its Truth into their lives and give themselves over fully to his teachings before they can attain all that they wish for.

In other words, "Buy my book, because you were always going to buy my book. And if in the end you don't get all the things you wanted out of life, well, that was never going to happen anyway." A bulletproof ideology, no risk and all reward. "*Riches are consistent with godliness, and the more a man hath, the more advantage he hath to do good with it,*" he wrote. Something told me Fear-Gods knew he was going to sell a lot of books.

The distance to Lincoln seemed longer than could be possible on a finite planet. Again and again I put the book down to stare out the window, only to snatch it up again minutes later and start thumbing through its pages. One word kept grabbing my attention, leaping off the page as if it had been highlighted – "Seneschal". Mortify had asked if I was going to see the Seneschal. I hadn't understood the question, but the word sounded familiar, as if I had heard it somewhere else in the recent past. "Seneschal" was the title Fear-Gods had given himself, as he explains:

> *"A seneschal was the steward of a great house in the Middle Ages, in charge of*

the administration of laborers and a royal officer responsible for dispensing justice. That is all that I am – an administrator. I administer the Word to a people hungry for meaning, for the Truth. I am no ruler. This mighty nation that is forming is one without monarchs, dictators, or presidents. No man can rule, only the Gods. To follow me is to follow them."

He was still the boss, in other words, but he didn't want to lord it over anyone. A utopia by nomenclature. I wondered what kind of situation Mortify was walking into.

We pulled into Lincoln long after sundown. I peered out the window, forgetting the book as I put all my attention into surveying the streets outside. There is something foreboding about an unfamiliar city after dark. Something primal, as if down every shadowy alleyway our minds perceive a sabretooth tiger lying in wait to pounce.

When we arrived at the station, I stood and gave the book back to Mortify, then started down the aisle. "What did you think?" he said.

I raised my eyebrows. "Interesting."

He grinned and made a strange sign with his right hand, putting the tips of his fingers to the corner of his eye. "Be seeing you." I frowned and nodded, saying nothing in return as I turned and left the bus for good.

Lincoln's Greyhound station was a corrugated aluminum shack on the outskirts of town, situated on the side of a four-lane highway lined with gas stations and cheap motels. A canvas banner that read "Bus Depot" sagged from the roof of the carport out front, looking like the sign for a roadside BBQ stand with its red lettering and yellow background. Across the highway, a sign for C&B Auto Sales presided over an empty grass lot where presumably cars had once sat. Empty metal frames towered above it all – billboard holders no company had thought it worth the cost to fill.

I stood by the side of the bus while the driver dug my bag out of the luggage hold, trying to plot my next move. Across the lot, a dozen or so school buses slouched beside each other in various states of disrepair. On my other side a freight facility squatted in a sea of asphalt, surrounded by a herd of truckless trailers gathering rust. It was a desolate, utilitarian place, all metal and concrete, as aesthetically bankrupt as anything the Soviet Union ever dreamed up.

Once I got my bag, I shuffled into the station and sank down onto the first seat I came to. An inspection of my wallet confirmed what I had already known – only nine dollars remained of the money I had taken when I left my apartment two days earlier.

Another three dollars and seventy-five cents were subtracted from that total when I bought a bottle of water and some cheese-filled crackers from the vending machines, gulping them down as if they were aspirin. As soon as the food began to settle, I felt the weight of the last few days come crashing down on me. Invisible hands tugged at my eyelids, refusing to let go. It occurred to me that I hadn't slept once since the strange dream I had had in my apartment while waiting to meet BB at the gym.

The waiting area was nearly deserted. The lone ticket agent on duty was busy with paperwork and paying no attention to what anyone else was doing. I picked a row of seats furthest from the counter, out of the agent's line of sight. Then I raised the armrests, stretched myself out across the cushions and drifted into unconsciousness, the TV hanging from the ceiling above me – where a local news anchor was describing a series of carjackings that had taken place across the northeast – playing me off to sleep.

Chapter 8

In the beginning there was nothing, and then there was pain – a searing, stabbing pain in my ribs that wrenched me from sleep and left me clinging to the backs of the chairs on which I lay. A uniformed security guard loomed over me. He bent down to get a closer look, frowning with distaste, as if I were a chewed-up wad of gum he was going to have to scrape off the cushions. In his hand was a baton, the end of which he rapped repeatedly against one of the seats.

"You habla English?" he shouted.

"Course he does," said a somnolent voice. I looked toward its source and saw another guard standing a few feet back, much shorter than the first and so skinny that his uniform hung from him as if he were a child trying on his father's clothes. "Look how white he is."

"Could be a European," said the first guard, jabbing the point of his baton into my kidney. I yelped and scrambled upright. The guard, a hulking man with the shape and demeanor of a concrete block, grabbed the back of my collar and hoisted me into the air like a mother cat lifting her kitten by the scruff. He leaned in close, breath stinking of stale coffee and breakfast sausage. "You European?"

"No," I croaked, trying to work the frog out of my throat. "American!"

He eyed me dubiously, then lowered me back onto the seat. He took his baton and stuck the point an inch from my nose, wagging it at me like a giant index finger, though no finger had ever terrified me half as much. "Listen good," he said. "You've got exactly two minutes to make a choice. Either grab your shit and hit the road, or Orville here and I drag you outside and use you as a training dummy till the cops show up to take you to jail."

I looked back and forth from the big guard to Orville, who stood in the background, his half-lidded eyes barely visible under a too-large hat. Orville shrugged. "He probably means it."

I nodded, squeaking out something I hoped sounded like assent. Disappointment soured the big guard's face, but he was a man of his word and allowed me to gather up my bag and scurry for the exit without further trouble. I shouldered the door open and scampered across the lot toward the road. Behind me, Orville and his partner stood in the open doorway, watching until they were satisfied I had left the premises and wasn't coming back. Passing through the gates at the parking lot's entrance, I turned and walked along the grassy berm of the highway in the direction I hoped would take me to downtown Lincoln, glancing back just in time to catch a glimpse through the chain link fence of the station doors swinging shut.

Lincoln's suburbs were as unfit a place to walk as most of America, as if they had been designed with active hostility toward anyone who couldn't afford a car. I staggered along, hoping for a street sign or mile marker, anything to help orient me. Those who did have cars rocketed past on my left, spraying me with exhaust fumes while I picked my way around streetlamps, fire hydrants, generators, mailboxes, and a host of other obstacles no city planner had ever considered a person on foot would have to navigate. It was late morning. The sun was getting higher, burning the dew off the grass and turning the air moist and heavy. Sweat beaded on my skin, working its way through the oily film that coated me head to toe. My head reeled, as if I'd been up drinking the night before. I looked around for a gas station or convenience store, anywhere I could buy another bottle of water, but now that I needed one they were mysteriously absent.

Reluctantly, I stuck out my thumb. Raised in the era that I was, horrific scenarios played themselves out on a reel in my head. I had never hitchhiked before. The very act of raising my thumb felt transgressive. Terror and excitement jockeyed for supremacy inside me. If there exists a finite number of ways one can be abducted and killed, my imagination failed to exhaust them. But I knew I had no other choice. Even if I managed to walk the rest of the way into Lincoln there was nothing I could do with only five dollars in my pocket. My only hope was to rely on the kindness of strangers, which is another way of saying no hope at all.

Or so I had thought. My hitching up to that point could be charitably termed "pro forma". I had not even bothered to turn and face the oncoming traffic, but continued plodding along toward Lincoln with my left arm dangling at my side, thumb perpetually extended as if my joints had fused that way. I was caught off guard then when a mint green Oldsmobile Ninety-Eight that had sped past me suddenly slammed on its brakes a quarter mile up the road and sat idling.

For a moment I stood and gawked, as if the car sitting there had nothing whatsoever to do with me. Then its horn began honking, and a hand reached out from the driver's side window to wave. Only then did it start to sink in that someone had agreed to give me a ride. I sprinted forward, afraid to lose this gift I'd been given before I had even received it.

The Oldsmobile sat clogging up the righthand lane like some mythic sea creature out of antiquity, the other cars on the highway like minnows clustered together as they scurried past on the left, a chorus of profanity issuing forth from their open windows.

The driver didn't seem to care. It was debatable whether he was even aware of what was happening. An oblivious grin greeted me as I clambered into the passenger's seat and shut the door. The driver introduced himself as Reginald, but "everyone calls me Reg," he clarified. He was in his forties, or thereabouts. A receding hairline had given way to full-on baldness, making it hard to determine his exact age. Only a few tufts of short, reddish-brown hair clung to the back and sides of his head, transitioning seamlessly into a scruffy, backpacker's beard of the same color. He had the soft, doughy build and slumped posture of a man who had spent his life working in offices. Empty fountain drink cups and fast-food containers littered the floor of the passenger's seat. Across the back seat, a snowboard sat propped against one of the windows.

"Hitchin'?" he said. I nodded, unsure if he was being rhetorical or not. Reg stuck his arm out the window and pointed straight ahead, like a general ordering his troops into battle. "Let's roll!"

Without turning or checking his mirror Reg thrust the Oldsmobile back out into traffic, weaving across both lanes. I flinched, but in vain; there was no great impact, no horrible crunch of plastic and steel. The sheer girth of the Oldsmobile was enough to keep the other drivers at bay.

Eventually, Reg committed to one set of lines and managed to keep the car more or less between them as we fell into the normal rhythms of the road. "Where you headed?" he said.

"West."

"Me too!"

I arched an eyebrow. "California?"

"Downtown. But I'd be happy to drop you off wherever." He gestured toward the back of the car. "Bus station's back that way, you know."

"That's ok," I said. "I've got no money."

Reg appeared to consider this, then nodded. As we approached downtown Lincoln, the dome of the State Capitol visible in the background, Reg pulled off the highway and turned onto a side street that meandered through a rundown residential area. After a couple blocks the street narrowed and the tattered houses that had lined it gave way to empty lots overgrown with weeds. We continued on, winding our way through scrubland dotted with wooded patches, the city disappearing in the rearview mirror. A few minutes later the road terminated in a gravel patch that acted as a sort of turnaround.

"Where are we?" I said.

"Railyard's right over there." He pointed. "Since you're broke, I thought maybe you could hop a train."

I got out and walked to the edge of the gravel lot to get a better view. Stretching out below me was a swath of land the size of Central Park, a miniature town wedged between downtown Lincoln and the suburbs. Two dozen rail lines sat side by side in a large hexagonal area, occupied by freight trains of varying lengths. Near where I stood was a narrow, dirt footpath sloping down to the yard below. I started to call back to Reg when I realized he had already swung the car around and was speeding away, kicking up a cloud of dust in his wake. Shielding my eyes, I caught only a glimpse of the back of the Oldsmobile as it rounded the corner and disappeared from view.

As the dust settled, I stood there, bewildered, as alone as a Gretel-less Hansel sulking in the woods. I considered returning to town, either to hitch another ride or to find a way to earn some money to buy a bus ticket. But the thought of walking all that way without any guarantee of success, coupled with the closeness of the trainyard, began to bring me around to Reg's suggestion. Americans had been hoboing for generations, I reasoned. It was hardly an outlandish idea. I decided to do some reconnaissance. Eschewing the footpath, I crept through the tall grass off to its side, staying as low as possible and peeking my head above the blades only when necessary to regain my bearings.

I expected to face a gauntlet of security measures – fences, barbed wire, cameras, sensors, alarm systems, armed guards, patrol vehicles, etc. But the yard seemed to be wide open, almost eerily so, as if it were trying to lure passersby into a trap. The closer I got to the tracks the more I braced myself for some sort of resistance, some seemingly impenetrable barrier I would have to navigate or else be forced to turn back. Perhaps a part of me was hoping for just that, a reason to declare defeat without feeling like I'd given up. If so, the trainyard provided no such excuse. In no time I had reached the edge of the grass and was only a short scramble from the nearest track, where a compact CSX train sat unattended as it waited to make the journey to who knows where.

That, as it turned out, was my biggest problem – I had no way of telling where any of the trains were going. I kept undercover and studied the CSX, as well as the engines and other cars I was able to see on the neighboring tracks, looking for some marking that would clue me in to their eventual destinations. The longer I sat and observed, I became aware that the yard was not totally deserted. From time to time an engineer or group of mechanics would appear, on their way to or from some job farther in toward the interior of the yard. But the trains on the outermost tracks appeared to be abandoned. Circling the perimeter until there was as little empty space as possible between me and the CSX, I waited until no workers were in the vicinity. Then I burst from the safety of the grass like a sprinter from his starting blocks, scurrying across the intervening space like some woodland creature being pursued by hounds.

On reaching the train I dove underneath the nearest car and lay flat on my stomach, taking long, deep breaths while I waited for my heart rate to slow. When the blood had stopped pounding in my ears I crawled over to the other side and peered out. Another, longer train waited on the second track. It too seemed to be unattended. Once again, I scanned up and down the line of cars, trying to figure out where the train was headed, with similar results. I weighed my odds. Was it smarter to hop into the first open car I found and hope it took me west, or keep working my way inward, checking each train until I found one that I knew was headed in the right direction? Given the ease with which I had made it this far, I decided to keep chancing it. Finding the coast still clear, I scrabbled out on my hands and knees before half-crouching, half-running to the next train, where I once again dove underneath.

The pattern repeated itself a third and fourth time. I continued to encounter no resistance as I made my way deeper into the yard, but I was still no closer to figuring out which train to choose. Now a new problem confronted me. Two empty sets of tracks separated the train I was under from the next train over. Worse still, I could hear the voices of a railroad crew nearby working on one of the lines. The distance seemed too great, the risk too high. I decided to backtrack. I rolled out from under the train in the direction I had just come from and stood up.

"Hey!" boomed a voice behind me.

I whirled around and saw – standing near the end of the train, a couple dozen cars away – the yard bull. He was waving his arm, a handkerchief he'd been using to mop the sweat from his forehead still clutched in his hand. A brass star pinned to the chest pocket of his uniform glinted each time the sun caught it at a certain angle. Put together, it resembled some strange hybrid of semaphore and Morse lamp, though I didn't need a decoder to figure out what message he was trying to send.

No sooner had the bull taken his first step toward me than I started running the other way, circling around the engine behind me into the next row. A moment later the bull appeared at the opposite end, knees bent and arms spread like a basketball player in a defensive stance, ready to block me from passing, though we were separated by hundreds of feet. This time I ducked beneath the car to my right and emerged one row over, only for the bull to appear again, increasingly out of breath and agitated that I apparently wasn't going to come quietly.

There was no sense repeating the same maneuver over and over. A yard that size likely had multiple guards, I knew. At any moment he could radio to them or even enlist one of the railroad crews to help surround me, at which point I'd have no chance of escape. One last time I circled back around the engine to the row I had just come from, only instead of stopping I sprinted across the tracks toward the center of yard. It must have taken the bull some time to realize what had happened. I was almost across the gap made by the two empty rail lines before I heard him shouting in the distance behind me, as he realized I had given him the slip.

When I reached the next train I didn't stop, but continued running with all my strength, desperate to build up as much of a lead as possible. Only vaguely was I aware of the workers down some of the rows I passed, prepping their trains before departure. I took no notice of whether they saw me or not. Passing the center of the yard where the longest trains were parked, I allowed myself to slow down for a moment and check the next row I came to. Finding it deserted, I turned and sprinted between two massive freight trains, each so long I couldn't see where they ended. I scrambled around, looking for any car that was open. I needed to conceal myself before the bull or one of the workers caught up to me.

Most everything I passed was a tanker or coal car, and the few shipping containers I saw were bolted shut. Just as I was despairing of ever finding a place to hide, a burgundy container car came into view. Glimpsed out of the corner of my eye, it appeared no different than the handful of other containers I had passed, the doors shut and presumably locked. Something about it, though, struck a chord within me. I slowed to a jog, then stopped, overcome by déjà vu. Turning around, I hurried back to the front of the car and studied it more closely. On the doors, stenciled in white, was the number 'XLJ 456427'. It was the container we had used to stash the moving truck back in Newark. Somehow I knew, even before climbing up onto the hitch and testing the door latch, that the container was still unlocked. I popped open one of the doors and peered inside. Everything was just as we had left it. Quickly, I slipped through the opening and shut the door behind me. For a moment I worried that I had just trapped myself, but the door had no automatic latch and I was able to push it open again without much effort.

With the door closed, I squeezed around the side of the moving truck to the interior of the car. Shielded now from immediate harm, the adrenaline began to drain from my body. The stress of the past few days weighed on me like a lead apron. I slumped to the floor, exhausted. Leaning back against the moving truck's bumper, I noticed for the first time how hot the container was. Vents near the top of each end allowed light to filter in, but the air remained stagnant and heavy. Rivulets of sweat wound their way down my face like mountain streams from a melting snowcap. The bottle of water I had drunk at the bus station seemed like a distant memory.

Cupping a hand to my ear, I pressed against the wall of the container. Footsteps could be heard on the gravel outside. They grew steadily louder, until I could hear them passing mere feet from where I sat. I tensed as the sound stopped, not daring even to breathe into the intervening silence. Moments later the steps resumed, moving off at a languid pace. They didn't sound like the footsteps of someone in pursuit. Before I could ponder it too deeply, a piercing whistle rent the air. A moment later the car around me shuddered, sending me sprawling onto the floor. With jerking stops and starts the train began to inch forward. I could feel the ground sliding past underneath me. The air around me stirred as we picked up speed. A breeze worked its way through the vents, growing in intensity as we left the trainyard and passed the outskirts of the city.

Now that the worst had passed, I turned my attention back to my surroundings. Behind me, the moving truck bounced lightly up and down on its suspension like a fidgeting child. Curious, I popped open the back door and climbed up into the cargo area. Thomas Bartholomew Bradford still lay face down on the floor, though it was clear he hadn't been idle during our time apart. Other than a few scratches around his head and chest he seemed to be in good condition. The same could not be said for the walls and floor of the cargo bay, however, which had borne the brunt of Bradford's twelve-hundred pounds. A delirious laugh escaped me as I ran my hand over their pockmarked surfaces, as pitted and mangled as any battlefield, and tried to guess what the rental agent might imagine had happened there.

Time passes slowly in a vacuum. Miraculous coincidence or not, my interest in the statue and the moving truck soon waned. I left the truck and climbed down to sit beside the pallets at the front of the car. There were two of them, each piled high with books divided into stacks of a few dozen copies that were shrink-wrapped in place. I wondered to myself who would pay the cost to send an entire shipping container across the country just to deliver a couple pallets of books. It was only a passing thought; my mind was too preoccupied with the heat to focus on much else. Even the breeze now circulating through the car felt like a hair dryer blowing on my face. I dragged my tongue uselessly around my mouth, searching for moisture. My body felt on the verge of collapse, yet no matter how I contorted myself I could not get comfortable.

Unable to sleep, I decided to read instead. I slid over to the pallets, felt along the surface of the shrink wrap until I found a small tear and ripped open a hole. The weight of the other books pressing down made it difficult, but I managed to wiggle one loose and pull it out from the stacks. Even in the dim light I immediately recognized the white cover with the blue bar running through the middle of it – *Providence's Blessing.* Hundreds of copies of it accompanying me westward. The car was too dim to make out the print. Spotting an area to my left where the sun's rays angled in through the vent, I slid over to it and leaned back against the wall, propping the book open on my knees. I skipped the prologue this time and chose a page at random from the middle of the book, hoping to distract myself from the fact that I had no food or water.

In Chapter 2, 'The Fatalistic Mind', Fear-Gods writes:

> *"As a child, years before my parents' deaths, I had a flip book. The book contained 65 pages, each one with an illustration. On the first page was a picture of a cartoon cat riding a bicycle. On the final page, the cat*

was prostrate on the ground, X's over his eyes and tiny stars spinning around his head, his bicycle upended and smashed against a tree. Flipping through the book from the first page to the last, I could see the events – each one a snapshot of a moment in time – that led to the cat's demise. Conversely, by flipping the book from the last page to the first, I could view the exact same snapshots in a different order – the bicycle now rebounded from the tree, mending itself in the process, while the cat's injuries healed themselves as he leapt from the ground onto the seat of the bike, pedaling it backwards up the road. That it did not matter in which order these snapshots were viewed was a thing I would not understand for many years. The cat had always ridden his bicycle. The cat had always crashed into the tree. Both would forever continue to happen and were happening simultaneously, just as both the first and last pages of the book existed simultaneously.

So it is with us, the eternal children of the Gods. Our lives are but images engraved in a book, never to be altered or erased. Trust in the Gods and strive to carry out their will, for in one's actions will be reflected the knowledge that one is of the elect. And if suffering befalls a man, he shall know that he is of the sullied. Such is the tragedy of the awakened conscience. It declares its own nothingness."

As I was about to turn the page a shiver passed through me. I turned. Two figures sat in the cab of the moving truck, emanating a soft, silvery light that wafted through the container like mist. Their long, expressionless faces gazed down at me on the floor. They remained as still as funerary statues. I couldn't tell if they were evaluating me or waiting for something, an explanation of some kind. I started to speak, but the figure in the driver's seat – the taller of the two – raised a hand to stop me. With a finger he beckoned me toward him, the truck door seeming to open of its own volition as I approached. Tentatively, I climbed into the cab, aware always of their eyes – teardrop-shaped orbs the absolute black of a dead universe – tracing my movements. No sooner had I settled in my seat than the door slammed shut behind me.

"You know us," said the taller one. It was not a question. All the same, I nodded. The tall one gestured toward the truck's dashboard. Right on cue the display lit up, growing brighter and brighter until the dials and meters started to melt and swirl together, forming at last a sort of silvery disc. "Look closely," said the shorter one. I peered into the center of the disc where an image was forming – an immense chamber of white stone, like something from an ancient palace. At one end of the chamber was a low table adorned with symbols, a sort of altar, on which was secured a bullet-shaped, metallic canister.

"Do you recognize it?" said the tall one.

"Not the room," I said. "I've never been anywhere like that before."

"What about the object?" said the short one.

I studied the image more closely. "It looks like some sort of bomb."

The tall one nodded. He gestured toward the silver disc, where the image had begun to transform. A vehicle of some sort was driving down a highway. It was a moving truck. Not the same truck we were sitting in, or at least it didn't look the same. Through the driver's side window, I could see that it was me behind the wheel. I was approaching a line of toll booths, past which I could make out the George Washington Bridge and the Manhattan skyline stretching across the background.

"What is this?" I asked.

"Keep watching," said the short one.

The image skipped ahead. I was in Lower Manhattan now, pulling into the entrance of City Hall Park. An event of some sort was going on. A podium has been placed at the top of the steps in front of the Hall, around which stood the mayor and other dignitaries. A modest crowd had assembled on the lawn. News vans were scattered about the property as well, around which a cadre of tanned and imperious reporters stalked, each trailed by a gaggle of bored-looking cameramen and production assistants. A security guard waved me through the gate, where I was met by a pair of police officers. They escorted me through the assembled crowd to a parking lot around the side of the building.

A group of workers from the Public Works Department joined me at the back of the truck as I opened the door and extended the ramp down to the ground. We were working together to take something out of the cargo area, something large and difficult to manage judging by all the equipment and coordination that was required. A wheeled cart, like a larger version of a dolly you might find at Home Depot, was rolled up the ramp and into the back of the truck. Moments later it reemerged, carrying a large, bronze object – the statue of Thomas Bartholomew Bradford.

After giving the workers a few final directions, I left them and scampered up the steps to join the mayor and other civic leaders on the rostrum. There was a smattering of applause from the crowd as I shook the mayor's hand. Then I stood off to one side while the mayor took his place behind the podium and adjusted the microphone. He was obviously preparing to give a speech. The mayor's mouth began to move, but I couldn't hear anything. It was as if I were surveying the scene from a distance, through one of those tower viewers you have to put a quarter in to operate. The mood onstage seemed lighthearted, even festive. The mayor had a wide grin plastered on his face. Several times he made side comments in my direction, one of which earned a hearty laugh.

After a minute or so I could see the line of officials in the background parting. The dolly holding the statue of Bradford was wheeled through the opening and onto the stage. The workers grasped the sides of the statue and propped it upright just behind where the mayor and I were standing. It towered over us, its severe expression aimed out over the assembled crowd as if accusing them all of some grave misdeed. The mayor turned and feigned surprise, staggering backwards and clutching at his heart while the crowd chuckled. Then, with a few closing remarks, he gestured to me and stepped aside so I could take his place at the microphone.

I raised a hand in greeting and waited for the audience to stop clapping. When everyone was settled, I spoke a few words into the microphone, ostensibly a thank you to the mayor and everyone who had welcomed me. Then I gestured toward the statue behind me. Immediately, the scene disappeared. A white light flashed in front of me, sending me recoiling into the corner of the truck's cab, hands clamped over my eyes. I held them there, echoes of the flash still pulsating behind my eyelids. After a minute or so had passed I parted my fingers and squinted through the cracks toward the dashboard, checking to see if the light had subsided. The silvery disc remained; however, where the image of City Hall had been there was now a mushroom cloud, an enormous pillar of reddish-purple fire billowing into the sky where it mingled with the clouds overhead, illuminating them like a second sun. Blast winds rippled outward from the explosion, sending concrete, trees, and other debris flying in all directions. All that remained was smoke and fire. Horrified, I turned to ask the two figures what it all meant, but there was no one there. I was alone again. When I looked back at the dashboard the image was gone too. Only the tiniest flicker of silver remained, which disappeared the moment I glimpsed it.

I remained in the truck for several minutes, still as a stone, listening, though for what I couldn't say. The only sound was the rhythmic clacking and occasional squeal of the train's wheels against the tracks that had been my constant companion since we first pulled out of Lincoln. Nevertheless, I kept still, waiting for something to happen, anything to put into perspective what I had just seen. I refused to accept the most obvious interpretation. Outside, the sun had fallen lower on the horizon. Only a pinprick of light now shone through the vent, making a tiny circle on the wall to my left that inched higher and higher every moment that passed, counting down the seconds till nightfall.

Chapter 9

When I awoke, I was ascending into the air.

Rather, the entire container was ascending. I could feel it swaying from side to side beneath me, unmoored from the Earth. I jumped down from the moving truck and crouched on all fours, back arched and clawing at the floor like a startled cat, trying to keep my balance. The copy of *Providence's Blessing* I'd been reading had fallen from my lap. It slid back and forth along the ground as if guided by an invisible hand, like the pointer on a Ouija board.

From outside came a metallic whirring sound. The container shifted again. Though it continued to sway, there now seemed to be a deliberate direction to its movement, a wide, clockwise arc. Moments later the swinging sensation stopped. I felt myself being lowered, until a sudden jolt from below sent me tumbling to the floor. I lay there in a heap, muscles weary from dehydration and lack of sleep, listening to the sounds of machinery and men shouting to one another outside.

How many times I slipped in and out of consciousness I can't say. No sooner would I come to and look around, reacquainting myself with the container and reconstructing the events that had led me to be confined there, than a bump or jolt of some sort would again rouse me from a slumber I hadn't realized I had entered and restart the whole exercise – a never-ending cycle of waking without interlude. Eventually, through the fog, my mind registered a new sensation – a vibration coursing through the floor below me and up through my body, rocking me back to sleep. When next I woke, I could tell I had been asleep for hours. Dried spittle crusted the corners of my mouth. I ran my tongue over my lips, so cracked and dry they felt reptilian. Nevertheless, I had regained enough energy to pull myself upright and remain awake. My limbs throbbed from lying motionless on the hard floor. I arched my back and stretched. The lens turned; the world drew into focus.

It was then that I again noticed the container vibrating. What I no longer noticed was the clacking of wheels against train tracks. I went to the doors, undid the latch and eased them open. This time, instead of the back of another train car, I saw miles of open road snaking across an arid valley. In the distance a line of rocky, snowcapped mountains dominated the landscape. The sun shone bright and cold against a cloudless sky, itself an icy, bloodless shade of blue. It was like no place I had ever seen before, which I hoped meant I was still headed west. The vibration was coming from the engine of the tractor-trailer that now towed me through this unfamiliar place. How long ago had I left the train, I wondered? I glanced down at the road as if I might find the answer there, right at the moment it began to curve. I lurched sideways, almost losing my balance. As soon as I had steadied myself, I slammed the door shut and bolted it again.

There are only so many things one can do in the back of a tractor-trailer to pass the time. Mostly I stared at the walls and hoped for a quick end to my journey, but obstinate as ever the truck continued on. For all I knew we could have been driving in circles, crisscrossing back and forth through the same barren valley hour after hour until the gas ran out and the truck's engine sputtered to a halt.

Assuming we ever run out of gas, I thought. Dark conspiracies began sprouting like crabgrass around the fringes of my mind. What if they knew I was back here? What if they brought a gasoline tanker up beside us to fill our tank while still moving, the way fighter planes refuel in midflight? Shuddering, I imagined being forever imprisoned in a moving cell, eternally bobbing and weaving, rising and falling over this bleak, alien terrain. It was an absurd thought, but my stomach churned and I could taste the bile pushing up into my throat. I thought about lying down and trying to rest some more, but was certain that if I did the truck would arrive at its destination while I was asleep, and I would be captured and handed over to the police.

My only remaining option was to pace about the trailer like a lunatic, letting my mind wander where it would. My thoughts went back to a restaurant my parents used to bring me to as a child, way out in the boonies of northern Pennsylvania, called The Farm. It really was a farm, in fact, a couple dozen acres of fields carved out of the Allegheny Forest where they grew corn and hay and soybeans. The farmhouse at the center of the property had been converted into a "family style" restaurant, serving burgers and hot dogs and pizza and all the other things kids will eat without complaining. Outside, surrounding the restaurant in a wide horseshoe, were pens filled with animals. For a quarter you could get a handful of dried corn kernels or grain pellets and feed the horses, cows, and goats. There were more exotic animals too – whitetail deer, peacocks, a bobcat, even a coati. But the animals most people flocked to see were the black bears. You could find them toward the top of the horseshoe. A separate, unmarked path tucked in behind the rooster and antelope pens brought you to their enclosure. It was not easy to spot – only those already in the know would have any idea what was back there – which made visiting the bears feel rather illicit, like slipping into a speakeasy or a backroom cockfight.

The first thing you noticed about the bears is that they were miserable. You did not have to be an animal behaviorist to see the pronounced sag in their expressions. They paced back and forth from one end of their enclosure to the other without pause, eyes round and watery like an infant's, unable to comprehend their own suffering. The pacing was the worst. First, know that their enclosure is not what you imagine. Picture a slab of concrete a foot off the ground, twenty feet long by thirty feet wide. Around the perimeter of the slab is a chain link fence. Another section of fence bisects the enclosure, dividing it into two equal spaces. In each of these spaces was a wooden hutch, barely big enough for the bear to squeeze into when it wanted to sleep or have privacy. Nothing else. Day after day the bears would wake, stumble to their feet and shuffle across the hard, concrete floor until their noses pressed against the fence, at which point they would turn around and do the same thing in the other direction. Over and over, until they collapsed from exhaustion. But something would always wake them – the heat (the enclosure was not shaded) or a sadistic visitor who thought it would be fun to pelt the bears with food pellets – and they would soon lumber to their feet once more and resume pacing. They resembled nothing so much as prisoners in solitary confinement, sent to their personal cages in the yard for their one hour of daily physical activity. Only in the bears' case, their time in the yard never ended. They would have given anything to be by themselves, away from the jeering crowds, from the children who giggled and gorged themselves on cotton candy while the bears slowly atrophied and slipped into madness. Even now their memory is like a lead weight pressing against my chest.

It took me two and a half steps to cross the width of the container. If I walked in a circle in the little area at the rear of the container, boxed in by the back wall and the moving truck, I could fit in six steps. Squeezing past the moving truck to the front of the container took another four long steps, while the tiny square near the pallets allowed me only enough room to spin in circles. I tried to keep to one part of the container as long as I could, devising new routes to follow and creating intricate patterns, until I had exhausted every possibility I could conjure in my diminished state. Then I would move on. After a while I reversed myself, using the patterns I had devised in the first area in the second area, and vice versa. In the beginning it seemed as if the possible combinations were limitless, but barely a half-hour in I had already run out of things to try. My mood was deteriorating by the second. On a whim, I got down on the floor and tried to do pushups, but my arms were too weak to even hold me upright in the starting position. I collapsed flat on my chest. The adrenaline that had been fueling me for so much of the trip had long ago dried up. I lay there like a discarded marionette, moving only when the whims of the road decreed it.

As the truck rounded a tight curve, the momentum rolled me sideways onto my back, arms and legs splayed out at angles like a cruciform. My eyes simmered as though they were sunburned, the lids fused together like suction cups. I used my fingers to pry them open and blinked repeatedly, trying to squeeze whatever moisture remained in my body up through my tear ducts.

As I blinked, images began to form and crystalize in front of me. Where the roof of the trailer should have been – where it *had* been just a few moments before, I was certain – a cityscape now loomed, filling the foreground. In the distance, just a pinprick on the horizon, a lone figure approached across a grassy field, dressed in a white cleric's robe that stood out against the dour background. The robe's hood was raised, obscuring the figure's face.

When the figure reached the city's outskirts, it stopped advancing. It raised its hands, grasped the sides of the hood and pulled it back. I was unsurprised to see that the figure was me. Some version of me, anyway. The color of my eyes was not quite right, a pale amethyst that looked unlike any human eye shade I had ever seen. There was a cold certainty in my expression – not arrogance, exactly, but a sort of righteous officiousness, like a bureaucrat carrying out his tasks cloaked in statutory authority. Dark clouds gathered in the sky above me. With a ceremonial flourish I raised my arms high above my head, muttering what seemed like an incantation of some sort. An eerie quiet descended. Even the sounds of the truck's engine and the trailer rattling over the highway had faded. The version of me in the image stopped speaking. There was no sound now, not even a wisp of breeze. Above, spots of light began to show through the clouds – soft at first, like the dull orange of a sunset, but growing ever more intense, until I could no longer bear to look at them directly.

Without warning, I thrust my arms down toward the ground, robe billowing around me with the force of the motion. From the clouds, six pillars of white light descended onto the city. There was a brief moment of silence as the oxygen was sucked from the air, turning the immediate vicinity into a vacuum. Then an explosion issued forth so powerful I cannot describe the sound it made. It was a thing felt rather than heard, rending my flesh, my connective tissue, dismantling me cell by cell. Everything the light touched was vaporized, while that which avoided direct contact nevertheless burst into flames and was consumed. In the aftermath, as the smoke cleared and the spots faded from my eyes, I could see skyscrapers reduced to sand, dispersing in the concussive winds the explosion had released. Further from the epicenter bodies lay strewn throughout the streets in various states of despair, burned to skeletons or, in a few cases, melted to the pavement as if made of wax. If anyone had survived the cataclysm, I did not see them.

Like a movie camera zooming out, the image began to widen, myself and the ruins of the city growing ever smaller as more and more of the surrounding landscape came into view. A river skirting the edge of the city, its banks altered by the blast, spilled its waters over the surrounding plains. Behind where I stood, miles of prairie stretched out like an ashen sea, charred by the superheated wind the explosion had unleashed. At the prairie's terminus, a row of granite peaks stretched across the horizon like the spine of some great beast, towering over the devastation in the foreground with solemn indifference. Above their snowy tops the sky itself appeared white, as if the clouds of smoke that billowed over the rest of the landscape would not dare to challenge their dominance.

The image continued to broaden, pull away. The robed version of myself was now barely visible, a tiny white dot being swallowed up by the immensity of the countryside. Even the city, reduced as it was, looked like little more than an abandoned campfire slowly burning itself out. Only the mountains retained something of their grandeur. I looked at them again, and to the strange, white sky above them. Something about the sky held my attention. The perspective was all wrong. It was almost as if it were behind the mountains rather than above them, a thing apart from the Earth itself. The more removed my point of view became, the more the whiteness began to take on physical characteristics. There was a texture to it, like fabric. It seemed to rustle and sway like a banner in a breeze.

The ground below had receded so far now that even the mountains could barely be distinguished. It was then that I noticed what seemed like a border of some sort encircling the landscape, as if outside a twenty-mile radius of the city the Earth simply fell away into nothingness. Looking back toward the whiteness, I saw now an undulating silvery light playing along its surface. All at once the sky was torn in two. The whiteness swirled and vanished in one violent motion, as if purged from existence. My blood ran cold. In its place, looming over everything, even the sky, was an enormous hand, its palm like a celestial dome surrounding the planet. The image pulled back further still, until I could see the arm and then the body of one of the figures who had visited me in my dream. The other figure stood just off to his side. They both looked down on the same scene I had been looking at, which I now realized was arranged on the surface of a table. The border I had seen was the table's edge, past which there was only emptiness and the two figures conferring together as they watched what transpired with passive interest.

The image vanished, replaced once more by the trailer's aluminum ceiling. I staggered to my feet and looked around, as if expecting the two figures and their table to be hiding in one of the corners. Somewhere, voices spoke – low murmurs that seemed to form out of thin air. There was an ethereal quality to them, as if I were overhearing snippets of a conversation from another dimension. I listened closer. The voices were coming from outside the trailer. Only then did it occur to me that the truck's engine was no longer running. We had stopped.

There was a 'thunk', and the trailer doors swung open. Sunlight poured in, as harsh and interrogative as a policeman's flashlight. Squinting through the glare I could see two men on the ground below me, their heads just visible above the trailer floor. The one nearest me had a dark mustache and wore a baseball cap. Above his eye a long, razor-thin scar rippled whenever he furrowed his brow. The other man stood a step or two behind the first, his head shaved and perfectly round; with his body obscured, he looked like a balloon bobbing just above the first man's shoulder. When they noticed me standing there they froze, then began speaking to one another in rapid-fire Spanish. Though I couldn't understand the words they used their tone alternated between annoyed and panicked. It was clear my presence had thrown a wrench into their day.

As their exchange grew more heated a note of determination entered the first man's voice. "Ok!" he said at last, one of the few words I understood. Roundhead fell silent, while Ball Cap turned and addressed me for the first time. "Come!" he said, beckoning me forward. "You, come!"

I hesitated. Ball Cap shot a glance at Roundhead, then looked at me again and repeated his command with renewed force. "Come, now!" he shouted. I took a single, cautious step forward. They seemed more nervous than threatening, but frightened men have been known to do terrible things. I had no idea where I was or whether anyone else was around. Would they get in trouble for letting someone stow away in the back of their truck, I wondered? Would it be easier for them to just abandon me in the middle of nowhere, or worse yet, kill me and dump my body out here, pretending like nothing had happened?

Their shouts continued as I took another step forward, delaying as long as possible while I sized up the situation. My options at that point were limited to running or fighting. I wasn't sure I had the strength for either. Perhaps I should surrender, I thought, make things as easy as possible for them. They might take pity on me, give me some food or water. As I neared the opening, the drivers' hands reaching out to seize me, a third voice – this one speaking English, and instantly recognizable – could be heard approaching in the background.

"You made it!" it said. Shouldering the drivers aside, BB stepped forward and leaned against the back of the trailer. Smiling broadly, he gestured over his shoulder. The ground behind him, stark white and perfectly flat, stretched into the distance without a single discernable landmark, as vast and uniform as a frozen sea. Sunlight shimmered on its surface as if it were made of diamonds.

"BB…" I said. "Where am I?"

"Where do you think?" he said, arms wide. "You're home!

BB took my hand and helped me down from the trailer, the drivers still eyeing me warily. The ground crunched beneath my shoes, as if I were walking on crushed glass. It was salt – miles and miles of it as far as the eye could see. The sun's reflection was blinding. I cupped a hand over my eyes while I waited for them to adjust. "Here," said BB, handing me a pair of sunglasses. "We all wear these."

I was in the middle of putting them on when BB took me by the shoulders and turned me around. "My God," I said. A massive, white palace stood just a few hundred feet away from us, blotting out the horizon. It looked like something the British Raj might have erected in India to cow the natives, a sprawling, neoclassical edifice projecting its might across the barren landscape. Aside from the palace, the delivery truck, and our little group milling about between them the whole world was flat and white. It was as if we were drawings that had managed to escape our two-dimensional world and now stood free upon the piece of paper on which we had been sketched.

Six large columns flanked the building's entrance, above which was a sculpture carved into the surface of the tympanum. Twelve figures in medieval dress stood side by side. Each one was engaged in a different occupation – a peasant harvesting vegetables, a court jester juggling balls, a knight leveling his sword at a fallen opponent, and so on. I recognized it almost immediately as the building I had heard described in *Providence's Blessing*, the palace Fear-Gods had seen in his dream. "What is this place?" I said to BB. He smiled and clasped my shoulder. "Better let you see for yourself."

Turning to the drivers, he said, "We'll send out a couple guys to help you unload this." Then he beckoned for me to follow him toward the palace. We trudged up the stairs side by side. "BB," I said, "are these steps made of salt?"

"The whole building is," he said. "There's nothing like it on Earth."

I looked up again at the enormous structure, newly awed. “How is it I never knew this was here? Why isn’t this place famous? There should people lined up for miles waiting to take pictures.”

“The Seneschal is concerned with secrecy.” BB shrugged. “Don’t ask me how he’s kept a lid on it for so long. I don’t have all the answers, I only recently arrived here myself, remember?”

We passed through the two innermost columns and then a double-door entryway of solid gold, propped open to receive us. Embossed on the inside of each door was the image of a skull with wings sprouting from its sides.

“I’ve seen this before,” I said.

“Yeah?” said BB.

“In a dream.”

BB nodded, as if this news squared with his understanding of things. We continued inside.

The palace had no foyer. Rather, on entering, one was thrust without fanfare into the Great Hall, a cavernous but spartanly decorated room. Imagine the Hall of Mirrors in Versailles without the mirrors or statuary and with every square inch of the walls and ceiling having been whitewashed.

“You said this was my home,” I said to BB, still craning my neck to take in all of the palace’s splendor.

"That's right. Didn't I tell you, man? We didn't have a plan, but I *told* you I'd get you there."

"Where?"

"Where you belong. Where the universe wants you."

"This is Fear-Gods' temple." I held BB's gaze, waiting for acknowledgment. He stared back, an impish grin on his face, then nodded. "He wants to meet you. He's been *waiting* to meet you." As he spoke, BB slinked backwards, gesturing in frantic waves for me to follow him.

We passed through the Great Hall and down a corridor into a smaller room that resembled a formal parlor, furnished lavishly and decorated in rich burgundies, golds, and greens. "He's right through there," said BB, in a strange, giggling voice, pointing toward a door at the other end of the parlor that led to a sort of antechamber. "Go ahead," he urged.

"Aren't you coming?"

"No, no…" BB looked down at his feet, wringing his hands. "He wants to see you alone."

"*He* wants…? How does he even know I'm here?"

BB began chuckling again, an unsettling, mirthless laugh. "It's like I told you before – everything we do, the universe reacts. You just have to learn to read the signals." He pointed again. "Go."

Then he backed out through the door from which we had just entered, closing it behind him.

I took my time crossing the room, pretending to admire the furniture and bric-a-brac scattered everywhere. When I finally reached the doorway of the antechamber, I paused and studied the interior. It was a tiny room. In the center was a round tea table with two chairs arranged face-to-face. In the corner was a kitchenette with a portable cooker, coffeemaker, and mini-fridge. On the far side of the room was another door, this one closed, made of heavy oak.

The sound of a door closing in the parlor behind me jolted me from my thoughts. Instinctively, I rounded the tea table and stood next to the chair on the far side. After a moment, a man entered the room. He wore a loose-fitting shirt with wide sleeves gathered at the cuffs, knee-length pants and a doublet overtop of a vest. A cape of jet-black silk hung from his shoulders. On his head was a felt hat, turned up at the front and adorned with a buckle. We made eye contact, and he smiled. “Hello, Edwin Block.”

I smiled back. “Hello, Fear-Gods.”

Chapter 10

The first minute was spent silently regarding each other across the table. Then, Fear-Gods said, "Would you like something to drink? You look thirsty."

I had forgotten how long it had been since I had had any water. At his words a dry, crackling heat seemed to spread across the inside of my throat. It was so parched I could barely speak without coughing. My voice croaked as I thanked him. Fear-Gods rose from his chair and went over to the mini-fridge, which was stocked top to bottom with bottles of water. He took one out and handed it to me. I tore off the cap and threw back my head, draining it in a matter of seconds. "May I have another?" I said.

Fear-Gods chuckled and retrieved a second bottle. When he had handed it to me, he remained at my side, placing his hand on my shoulder. "You know," he said, "those who serve here in the Temple address me as Seneschal."

I paused in the middle of a long swallow and took the bottle from my mouth. "Sorry," I said. "I didn't mean any offense." As I spoke, I could feel his fingers pressing into my shoulder, going ever deeper, digging through the tissue until the tips ground against bone. I winced. Suddenly, he released me, patting me on the back before returning to his seat.

"Not to worry," he said. "All titles are as nothing before Them."

My shoulder stung, but I ignored it and held his gaze. "You mean the men in white."

Fear-Gods studied me, his eyes like coals. "Do you know why you're here?"

"No." I set the bottle on the table. "I know you were expecting me. At least that's what I was told."

"Yes…" He leaned back in his seat, regarding me the way a New York art critic might the work of some high-flown rube from the sticks who had just discovered abstract expressionism. "That *is* true. I knew you would arrive here someday, though I admit I didn't know when. It could have taken you years to find your way." A triumphant grin twisted the corner of his mouth. "But you're here now."

"And where is here?" I said. "What is this place?"

"This," he said, with a sweep of his hand, "is the culmination of a life's work. All the tragedies I've suffered, the abandonment, the heartache…" He paused for a moment as his breathing grew shaky, face clenched as if reliving some traumatic moment from his past. Then gradually he began to relax again, his expression regaining its intensity. "And then my revelation! My communion with the Gods. The years of wandering and learning, of writing and preaching the Truth to the peoples of the world. All of it has gone into this building. It is my home. It is a temple, a sign to our Gods that we hear and obey them." Reaching across the table, he laid his hand on mine. "That is why you're here," he said. "You've been chosen."

"Chosen?"

"The *men in white*, as you call them. I know you've had visions. I know that they've spoken to you." His eyes grew wider. "You must do as they say."

Hesitantly, I shook my head. Fear-Gods gripped my hand tighter. A crazed look came over him. "There is no choice, do you understand? It is your destiny, you must comply!" This time I pulled away from him and leapt up from the table. "Forget it," I said.

"You must!"

"The things they showed me…"

Fear-Gods stopped and considered me for a moment. "They disturbed you?"

I did not respond, but the answer must have been plain on my face. Fear-Gods relaxed his posture and gestured for me to sit down. "Please," he said. I approached the table, warily, and sat. "You've read my book?" he asked.

I nodded. "Some of it."

"There are things I did not include there," he said. "Whether out of vanity or the sincere concern that they might distract the flock from hearing fully the power of the Word, there are things about my youth I decided not to include." A button was coming loose on the sleeve of Fear-Gods' shirt; he fondled it aimlessly with his thumb and forefinger as he spoke. "Do you remember the scene where I described my revelation, the first time the Gods appeared to me and showed me what my fate would be?"

"After your parents died," I said. A slight tremor, almost imperceptible, passed through Fear-Gods' face. He nodded. "It's true, what I wrote. My mind really was opened by what the Gods showed me. I really did lead the detectives through the house and answer their questions with preternatural calm. But a week later…" He took a deep breath, as if to brace himself. "A week later, at my aunt's house – she was the one who took me in after my parents died – I was getting dressed in my bedroom. It was the morning of my parents' funeral. One funeral for the both of them, the bodies laid out side by side. Forced to act out in death the same charade that had ruined their lives…"

Fear-Gods' jaw clenched, a brief expression of anger that he concealed almost as quickly as it had surfaced. "The following day my aunt and I had an appointment with Child Protective Services to begin the process of her formally adopting me. I was looking in the mirror, trying to fasten a tie for the first time in my life, when suddenly I just gave up. I didn't want any of it – my parents' deaths, a new life with my aunt…least of all the burden the Gods had placed on me. I grasped the tie…" Here, Fear-Gods began miming with his hands. "I wrapped it around my neck, forming a crude noose, and cinched it tight. Then I went over to the bed and climbed onto it. It was a tall bed, an antique, with an iron frame and a headboard that stretched halfway to the ceiling. I fastened the other end of the tie to the very top of the bedpost." Again, he mimicked tying a knot. "Then, I stood on the edge of the mattress, my toes dangling out over the void, and looked down at the floor. It seemed like it was miles below me. I closed my eyes and marshalled every negative thought my damaged psyche could conjure. With a final rush of conviction, I took a step forward and felt myself drop. The last thing I remember was how quickly it all went. I barely remember falling at all, just the slack tie going suddenly rigid and a pleasant warmth rising up through my body, as if I were submerging myself in a bath. The next thing I remember was waking up in a bed in the child psychiatric unit at St. Anastasia Memorial Hospital."

"You were committed?" I said.

"Just kept for observation and then released to my aunt." Fear-Gods' eyes grew distant, gazing back through time. "They chalked it up to the trauma of discovering my parents. But it wasn't. It was *fear*. Fear of what lay in store for me, of the lines that had been penned for me in Destiny's book. I shrunk from it, the awesome responsibility. And so, I vowed to kill myself. Next, I tried cutting my wrists. I bought a package of razors, popped out one of the blades and plunged it deep into my skin without the slightest hesitation. Everything went black. But the next day I woke up back in the hospital. Apparently, I had missed my veins and cut straight into the flesh. They held me longer that time, but eventually I was released to my aunt."

A wry smile played across his face. "Then there was the time I threw myself off a bridge. I grabbed the guardrail, hoisted myself up onto the concrete barrier and flung myself over the edge…right onto the upper-deck of a passing ferry. I sprained an ankle but was otherwise fine. Next, I stole a handgun from a friend's house and tried shooting myself; the firing pin had been removed. I threw myself in front of an oncoming car; the driver was drunk and swerved off the road, right into the spot where I had been standing seconds before. Then I tried a train; I waited by the side of the tracks for an entire day, but none ever came. Someone had called in a bomb threat, and the line had closed down for a week. One time I stole my aunt's keys, went into the garage at night, started the car, and went to sleep; her cat knocked the automatic opener off the counter and onto the ground. It landed right on the button. When I woke up the next morning the door was wide open, exhaust fumes spilling out into the air.

On and on it went. I tried drinking myself to death, overdosing on drugs, picking fights in dangerous neighborhoods, asphyxiation, drowning, burning, impaling myself. Nothing worked. That was when I understood – I was trapped. The Truth the Gods had shown me was incontrovertible. I stopped fighting. I began listening to the universe, following its cues. For the first time everything began to make sense. The things that happened to me were not random, meaningless incidents – they were breadcrumbs scattered deliberately for me to follow. The trail led me to write my book. It led me to gather my flock, to bring them here to Utah where we built this palace. But that's not all…"

Fear-Gods rose from his seat and rounded the table. I tensed, thinking he was advancing upon me, but instead he passed around behind my chair and went to the oak door. He grasped the iron latch with both hands and forced it open. There was a clank, and the door swung inward. A warm, dry breeze wafted over me from the other room. “I have something to show you,” he said, gesturing for me to follow.

I had expected to find another room like the parlor we had just passed through. Instead, we emerged into a chamber nearly as large as the Great Hall itself, the walls made of the same salt bricks that formed the palace’s exterior. Carved into the walls were a series of symbols – the same winged skull I had seen on the doors; a willow tree beside an urn; a pair of hands, clasped; an hourglass with wings; a torch; an open book; a snake eating its tail. I took them in one by one as Fear-Gods led me through the chamber. If there was a larger, unifying meaning behind them I couldn’t understand it. I was about to ask him what they meant when he pointed to something I recognized immediately – an altar, adorned with many of the same symbols that were on the walls. Resting on top, held aloft and secured in place by a metal rack of sorts, was the warhead I had seen in my dream.

“It can’t be,” I said.

Fear-Gods beamed, as if he were showing off a new sportscar he’d just purchased. “Not an easy thing to obtain, I assure you. It took years and all the available manpower at my disposal to track down a reliable broker who could facilitate such a purchase. And the cost! You wouldn’t believe it if I told you. In the end we managed to locate an ex-Soviet general with access to a weapons cache that was stolen back when the communist government had collapsed. We met in Bulgaria, on the Black Sea, settled on terms, and the bomb was transported to a warehouse in Sofia. After that it was up to us to smuggle it into the United States. That was an ordeal in and of itself. But of course, our success was preordained." He winked and gestured toward the bomb. "Go ahead, take a closer look."

Revulsion and desire warred within me. I felt as if I had been given permission to satisfy some base perversion in full public view. In front of me was a device with the power to annihilate an entire city. And yet, lying inert on the altar, it looked practically domesticated, like a coffeemaker or kettle turned on its side. I inched closer, taking soft, deliberate steps, as if the bomb were a sleeping tiger that might awaken at the slightest sound. When I was within arm's length my hand instinctively reached out toward it, but Fear-Gods stopped me. "Not yet!" he said. "For now, just a quick look. I wanted you to understand the gravity of the role that's been given to you."

"I can't be involved in this," I said.

"You're afraid." He nodded. "That's understandable. But know that we're not just throwing you into this blindly. This isn't our first action. Just this week one of our cells successfully hijacked and brought down a passenger plane flying out of Boston. It was a test of our ability to coordinate and carry out large-scale operations. Needless to say we passed with flying colors, if you'll pardon the pun."

He clasped his hands behind his back and began to pace in a wide circle around me. "Your mission has been in development for much longer. Every detail has been painstakingly thought out, every contingency planned for. The Gods have been unusually explicit in their instructions. They are disappointed in us, humankind. They gave us dominion over the Earth and look what we've done with it."

"I thought that everything was already written," I said. "Aren't they the ones making the decisions, not us?"

Fear-Gods shrugged. "It hardly matters. If the Gods deem it necessary that humans should fail as a step in our evolution, so be it. The fact remains that they are displeased, and we must be punished." He stopped his pacing and approached me, placing his hands on my shoulders. "You have nothing to fear. Fate is on your side. This is to be the opening salvo in a revolution that will remake civilization from the ground up."

"If the Gods are so enlightened, why didn't they just choose the right path for humankind to follow in the first place?"

"It is not for us to question Their workings!" Fear-Gods thundered, pressing in on my shoulders as if I were a milk carton he was trying to crush. "You would presume to criticize the methods of a power beyond your comprehension? Seek not outside the way. If some have to die so that humanity as a whole can ascend to its full potential, then so be it. The Gods allow no evil that has not already been determined to end in good."

"It's still evil," I said, shaking free of his grasp. "I won't do it."

Fear-Gods' face flashed red. I braced myself, expecting him to strike me, but as quickly as it had been kindled the anger drained out of him. He seemed to deflate, his posture growing crooked, his breathing slow and labored. Sadness weighed on him like a yoke as he nodded his head. "I understand how you feel, Edwin. It isn't fair, you're right. For years I resisted, just as you resist now. I cannot begrudge you that. You have not seen all that I have seen." There was the briefest of pauses, during which Fear-Gods raised his eyes to meet mine. "I have something to show you."

"Another bomb?"

"Please, trust me."

The desperation in his voice disarmed me. I fell in line behind him as he scuttled off across the hall, back in the direction we had come from. Passing the door to the antechamber, we continued on to the opposite side of the room, where another door was set into the wall. I waited as Fear-Gods fiddled with the latch. "Perhaps this is something I should wait for the Gods to show you, when the time is right," he said. "And yet, some impulse compels me. Maybe that in itself is their signal that you are ready." The latch turned. He pulled the door open, standing off to the side and gesturing through the portal. "In here, you will find the answers to your questions."

I peered through the doorway. Nothing could be seen of the room beyond. It was as though the doorframe formed a barrier past which no light could enter or escape. Even as I approached the threshold the blackness was unabated. "Courage," said Fear-Gods, placing a hand on my back. A voice in my head told me to turn back. If there was something in the room that would convince me to go along with a plan as murderous as Fear-Gods', better to shield myself from it. But the mere possibility that something so persuasive existed was itself seductive. Curiosity getting the better of me, I stepped through the door.

Even inside the room the darkness was difficult to penetrate. As my eyes began to adjust, I saw that the room was round and of modest size, the walls the same salt-brick as the larger chamber we had just left. The ceiling extended far beyond even the Great

Hall's. Gazing upwards, I saw that I was standing at the bottom of something like a castle tower. A pale shaft of light entered through the room's only window, illuminating a spot on the opposite wall several stories above me. That accounted for the darkness. As strange as the configuration was, something else was gnawing at me. I stepped further into the room, feeling my way through the gloom until I had searched every inch of the interior. There was nothing. No furniture, no decorations, no books or artifacts or objects of any kind.

Behind me, the door slammed shut. Darkness enveloped me, as if a sack had been pulled over my head. I called out to Fear-Gods but there was no answer. My heart raced. Frantically, I groped my way through the blackness, trying in vain to find the exit. I stumbled, unable to draw breath; it felt as though an invisible hand were crushing my chest. There was nothing in the room with which to orient myself. I spun, impotent, through the void, arms flailing. Sweat beaded on my skin, which tingled as though it were being run through with an electric current. At last I found the wall and followed it around the circumference of the room, until I felt the rough salt bricks change to polished oak. My hands scrambled for the iron latch and tested it, but to no avail – it would not yield. I did not bother calling out again. Turning around, I fell back against the door and sank to the ground, the fight draining from my body. I was a prisoner.

Chapter 11

Feeding time was twice a day.

That was my assumption, anyway. The person who brought my food – not Fear-Gods, judging by his voice – would alternate saying "Breakfast time!" or "Dinner time!" with each meal. In the beginning, I had no choice but to take his word for it. Over the days and weeks that followed, however – time spent staring up at the window above me – I became more adept at surmising the hour from the angle of the light entering my chamber. At "breakfast time" the light shone through at about 15 degrees from center, while at "dinner time" it was more like 75 degrees.

Unfortunately, the food options displayed no such precision in conforming to cultural norms. I was just as likely to be given a greasy brick of microwave lasagna for "breakfast" as I was a rubbery stack of mini pancakes for "dinner". The meals were slid into my cell along the floor through a panel built into the bottom of the door. It was an ingenious contraption, simple as you like to open from the outside but impossible to budge even a millimeter from within. I can attest to that last point; I spent every waking hour of my first two days as a captive trying to pry it loose. If not for the fact that my fingernails had ground down past the nail beds and begun bleeding, I would have kept right on trying.

They laced my food with drugs.

Hallucinogens of some kind. Hours after my first meal a blissful sort of dreaminess settled over me like a warm blanket. I sat back against the wall, which had become as pliable as a couch cushion bending to fit the contours of my body. My eyes panned across the room, forcing the darkness to recede while my mind sketched in its place the intricate details of a carnival, a kaleidoscopic blur of flashing lights and whirling rides. As my gaze drifted upwards toward the window, I saw swooping in and out of the light shaft an enormous Luna moth, dipping and soaring in an endless figure-eight while silver dust fell from its wings like midwinter snow, blanketing the floor of my cell.

I'm not sure exactly when the men in white began appearing in my visions. One moment I was scrambling for safety as a mysterious, golden blob pursued me around the room, oozing over the floor like lava, and then suddenly they were there, seated beside one another on a stone bench and surrounded by their ever-present aura of swirling, silver light. The taller one pointed a finger at the blob; it emitted a blood-curdling scream, like a fisher cat's, and rose into the air. Suspended there, it widened and flattened until it became a sort of screen on which appeared yet another image of me striding triumphantly through a city in flames, followed by a throng of white-robed adherents. Little by little the men in white came to dominate my hallucinations, which were practically continuous by this point, harping always on the same old theme.

"You are the eagle, swooping down, spreading your wings over the Earth," said the tall one, in a typical diatribe. Between the two figures, in the background, a white horse fidgeted and tossed its mane impatiently. "You are the Comforter, the Counselor of men. Unleash tribulation; the flesh counts for nothing."

The sleepless hours piled up, one upon the other, like grains of sand slowly burying me. I sat slumped over like a narcoleptic in mid-seizure, unable to endure the barrage of apocalyptic imagery any longer. "What is it you want from me?" I slurred.

"We have already shown you," said the short one.

"The bomb?" I said. "You want me to deliver it to New York, and what? Detonate it?"

They nodded.

"What happens then?"

The short one shrugged. "What usually happens when a bomb is detonated?"

I shook my head, unwilling to accept the sentence I was being given. "What if I don't go?" I said.

"What if no matter what happens to me, I refuse to go to New York?"

The tall one laughed. "But you do go. It has already happened. Telling you this was required of us, and taking the bomb to New York is required of you. In fact, had we not told you all of this, you might never have gone to New York at all."

"Then why tell me?"

"Because we have always told you," said the short one.

"But you're Gods!" I said. "You can do whatever you want!"

They shook their heads in unison. "The people here call us Gods, but that is not what we are. We are simply visitors. Even we must play our parts."

A sudden inspiration seized me. "What if I kill myself? End things right now, so there's no way I could blow up all those people."

"You could try," said the tall one. "In fact, you do. But it doesn't work. You'll have a pang of conscience and convince yourself that suicide is cowardly, and that you can do more for the world if you stay alive and keep fighting. It's not true, of course. But since you deliver the bomb to New York, it's impossible to die before you do." He shrugged. "It's all very simple."

"So that's it?" I said. "There's no way out? I have no choice in the matter?"

"Of course you have choices," said the short one. "It's just that you've already made them."

"Then what is life for? Why do we keep reliving the same moments over and over? What is the point of all this?!"

They smiled. "We knew you were going to say that."

Chapter 12

My ordeal went on for six weeks, by my calculations. It could just as easily have been six months; the relative worth of my calculations is up for debate. There began to be a noticeable pattern in the visions I was seeing – the men in white would appear with their horse and order me to spread my wings over the Earth; we would argue about the bomb; they would tell me my fate was sealed and wink out of existence; ripples of green energy, like the northern lights, would snake through the room; and finally, there would be a creaking sound, a bang, and a meal would be shoved through the door slot. Every time the latter happened, I was certain that I had just been fed a few minutes earlier and would look around for the untouched plate. But it would not be there, only the new plate, which itself would not be there ten minutes later when the sequence repeated.

Bit by bit I began to unravel. I tried closing my eyes, but nothing changed. The visions continued unabated, as if my eyelids were transparent. I tried focusing my thoughts elsewhere, but the hallucinations were too powerful. The more I fought the harder they pressed in on me, forcing their way into my consciousness.

One by one, the threads began to snap. I felt myself growing disconnected from the physical world. The memory of what normality felt like was being erased from my mind. I decided to end things, before I lacked even the mental faculties necessary to formulate such an idea.

There were no objects in the room, as I've said, only the stack of empty paper plates no one ever bothered to come and collect. There was not even a toilet, only a floor grate along the wall, its dimensions no bigger than an envelope's. The smell must have been terrible, though in my altered state it made no impression on me. A small blessing, I suppose. With options so limited the only plan that came to mind was a hunger strike. I would starve myself to death.

When the next plate of food – pancakes – was shoved under my door, I pushed it to the side and refused to eat. Using every ounce of willpower, I kept my eyes focused on it, refusing to let it vanish as the others had.

From somewhere behind me the voices of the men in white could be heard intoning their ceaseless mantra: "You are the Comforter, the Counselor of men. Unleash tribulation; the flesh counts for nothing."

I did my best to ignore them and focus on the plate. Yet even as I did, I could hear myself speaking, mouth moving against my will: "What is it you want from me?"

"We have already shown you," came the response.

The plate of pancakes began to quiver, then pulse, as if it were a beating heart. "The bomb?" I heard myself say. I clenched my jaw and tried to prevent my mouth from opening, but the pulsating only became worse.

"What usually happens when a bomb is detonated…?"

The pancakes became more erratic. They thrashed and squirmed about the plate like a wild animal trying to free itself from a sack. "But you're Gods!"

Their dimensions began to change, stretching and pulling at their own boundaries as they grew steadily larger, as if the sack they were fighting to escape was space-time itself. I balled my hands into fists and furrowed my brow, redoubling my efforts to keep the plate of pancakes intact, but it was becoming a losing battle. I felt myself flagging.

"…even we must play our parts…"

The stack of pancakes grew taller, widening at the top. With every spasm of movement tufts of silvery light emanated from its surface. A definite shape began to emerge, vaguely humanoid – I could see the beginnings of a head, arms, legs. What was happening was clear, but I was powerless to stop it. "What if I kill myself?" I said.

All at once, as if being birthed, the men in white emerged before me fully formed, the plate of pancakes that had been there before seeming to melt out of existence. Once more they gazed down at me, their pale horse pawing the ground behind them.

"You could try," they said.

The loop reformed, unbroken. There was no way out.

"But it doesn't work."

Was it pointless to fight, I wondered? After all, I had delivered the bomb to New York. I had detonated the bomb. To change that would be to change the future. Did I have that right? What did I know of the future?

"You'll have a pang of conscience…"

They only said that I detonate the bomb. They never said what would happen when I did. There would be damage, of course. People would certainly lose their lives. But I could mitigate the damage. I could do everything possible to control the blast, to limit the fallout. The universe would be placated, but I would have saved countless people. I would be a hero.

"…you'll convince yourself you can do more for the world if you stay alive and keep fighting…"

Men are deluded, prone to a multiplicity of deceits. They are not convinced of the Truth, nor of their duty to submit to it.

"You deliver the bomb to New York..."

They are ready to bring their principles to agree with their practices, rather than the other way around. They paint false glosses on the Gods' teachings to bend them to compliance with their own desires.

"You deliver the bomb to New York..."

They believe all deluding flatteries, think themselves wise when they are fools. They think themselves beautiful when inside they are as a grave, a hellish vault inhabited by every foul demon and spirit.

"You deliver the bomb to New York..."

There is no plainer Truth than that eternal things are greater than temporal things. How reasonable, considering the Gods are wise and just, to suppose the future rewards those who follow their teachings? There is nothing more manifest or demonstrable than the being of God. It is in every corner to which we train our eye – the heavens, the earth, the air, the seas. And yet how willfully man embraces blindness!

"You deliver the bomb to New York..."

My eyes are opened. I submit to the awful frowns of Heaven and supplicate the Gods to wield me as a knight wields his sword.

I will deliver the bomb to New York.

A shudder passed through me. Strange colors continued to flicker at the edges of my vision, but the men in white were gone. There were no plates scattered across the floor, no human waste piling up by the wall. Blessed silence filled my ears, as beautiful as any music man had composed.

I lurched to my feet, limbs knotted and sore, and limped over to the door. Placing my hand on the latch, I pressed down. With a clank, the bolt slid free. The door swung open, waves of light washing over me. I stood propped in the doorframe for several minutes, my face buried in the crook of my arm. As my eyes began to adjust I could make out a shadow standing in front of me, one that eventually coalesced into the shape of a man whose voice gave him away even before I could make out his face.

"Come on," said BB. "It's time."

Chapter 13

Wide-open vistas drifted past my window, moving west to east this time. Lush, green grasses stretched out from the edge of the highway, giving way to arid scrubland that marked the boundary of the river basin through which we now passed. In the far distance, jagged, blue-gray cliffs loomed, silent and totemic. We rode along in silence. BB gazed placidly at the road ahead, unperturbed by the cars weaving around us like angry hornets as the moving truck chugged along, obstructing the right-hand lane.

The previous days had been spent resting and recovering my strength while the plan was being finalized. BB was the one who had filled me in on the details. I never saw Fear-Gods again.

The moving truck had been repainted to look like a New York City Parks Department vehicle. The New Hampshire license plate BB had removed had been replaced with a decommissioned one from New York. The VIN had been altered and fake registration and insurance docs had been created. In the back of the truck, surrounded by the requisite landscaping equipment and tools, was the statue of Thomas Bartholomew Bradford, a nuclear warhead embedded in its chest. The warhead was fitted with a remote detonator linked to a small, handheld triggering device – simply turn a key, flip a switch and press a button, and all of Lower Manhattan would be erased. The triggering device was in the side pocket of my cargo pants, flapping lazily against my thigh.

The plan was simple, unnervingly so. A contact that Fear-Gods had cultivated in the Parks Department's administrative pool had added a bogus statue installation at City Hall Park to the work schedule, assigning the job to our fictitious crew. All we had to do was drive through the night, appear at City Hall Park the following morning and security would wave us straight through the gates. Once we were on the grounds, we were to wheel the statue out from the back of the truck, stand it upright and then immediately detonate the bomb.

"Why stand up the statue first?" I said to BB. "You know how long that could take? What if someone gets suspicious?"

"That's just the plan, man," said BB, as sanguine as ever.

"I don't understand why we're even bothering to take it out of the truck. It's not like an aluminum box is going to dampen a nuclear blast."

BB shrugged. "That's how the universe wants it, I guess."

We didn't speak much after that. All the way through the Rockies and across the Great Plains BB and I stared out the window, the only voices in the cab those of AM talk radio hosts spouting conspiracy theories and hawking diet supplements with equal amounts of urgency.

It was turning eight o'clock as we barreled past Chicago and pushed over the border into Indiana. The sun was low on the horizon, casting a red-gold sheen that infused our otherwise mundane surroundings with an air of significance. "I've got to take a piss," said BB.

At the next exit we veered off the highway and descended into a wooded valley, pulling into the parking lot of a gas station situated at the bottom of the ramp. While BB went inside to use the restroom, I gassed up the truck. The sounds of the highway above were softer now, a white noise ebbing and flowing like gentle ocean surf. Aside from us and the lone cashier working the register the station was deserted. After a few minutes, BB joined me outside. We leaned against the cab for a while, watching in the distance as the streetlights of the nearest town blinked to life one by one.

"This is the end of our story," I said. "You know that, right?"

BB kept his gaze fixed on the lights, not responding.

"The remote trigger won't work at a distance of more than a couple hundred feet," I said. "We're going to be right next to it when it blows."

He shrugged. "We'll die instantly, at least. That's not nothing."

"Is this what you imagined when you suggested we take a journey?"

BB snorted, the corners of his mouth twisting into a grin. After a moment's pause, I said, "Whatever happened to your parents?"

A flicker of something crossed BB's face, too quick to read. He stood up straight and stepped away from the cab, spitting onto the pavement. "Come on. We've got to stay on schedule." We got back in the truck, our unspoken vow of silence renewed, and returned to the highway.

Ohio and Pennsylvania passed by in darkness. By the time the sun had risen the following morning we were in New Jersey, passing signs for the Oranges and Paterson and glimpsing in the distance the Passaic River, on whose banks we had abandoned the same moving truck only a couple months earlier. We continued on through Bergen County, past Hackensack and Teaneck, until finally we joined a mass of cars being herded together like livestock as they funneled through the toll booths at the entrance to the George Washington Bridge. As we joined a line and inched forward toward our appointed booth, I began to panic. Dozens of scenarios played out in my head, each one ending with our truck being searched and BB and me being led away in handcuffs. Our guilt seemed to me to be apparent, as if the words "Bomb Inside" had been painted across the sides of the truck. But when our turn came the attendant merely asked for our toll. We handed him $15, and he ushered us onto the bridge without so much as a second glance.

The tension grew as we crossed the Hudson and plunged down off the bridge into Harlem. FDR Drive was surprisingly clear as we sped the last few miles toward Lower Manhattan. Some sort of struggle would have seemed appropriate, a test that we would have had to overcome against all odds in order to cement for posterity that our triumph was inevitable, that we really were the chosen ones. Instead, we were barely spared a glance, so insignificant that even the police cruiser concealed beneath the Williamsburg Bridge paid no mind when we drove past it doing 20 miles an hour over the speed limit.

It was about that time that I truly started believing we might succeed. Despite the constant protestations from BB, my visions and the ordeal in Fear-Gods' temple, there had remained a nagging anxiety, a voice in the back of my mind sowing doubts about what we had set out to do. As we took the exit for the Civic Center, however, a penetrating calm filled my body, a deep peace like one experiences upon waking from a terrible dream and realizing that one is outside it all and cannot be touched by its imaginary phantasms.

The feeling stayed with me as we turned onto Chambers Street, then onto Broadway and the entrance to City Hall Park. The sidewalks were swarming with pedestrians on their way to work. BB swung the front of the truck in toward the park gates and inched forward, carefully parting the sea of people until we had managed to push through and dam off the flow altogether. Looking out my window at the faces waiting impatiently to get by us, I wondered where they would be when the bomb detonated. Who knew how long it would take for us to get inside the park, drag the statue out of the back of the truck and find a way to stand it up? Some of these people would probably be well outside the blast radius by that point. Others would be underground, riding the subway. Still others, it was certain, would be instantly killed.

A guard in a crisp, white uniform climbed down from his booth and ambled over to us. BB rolled down his window, handed the guard his identification and told him we were here for the statue installation. The guard scanned the ID disinterestedly, went back to the booth and checked a clipboard, then emerged again and went over to the gates. After a couple seconds of fiddling with the locks, the gates swung open and the guard waved us inside. BB eased the truck through the entrance, releasing a torrent behind him as the crowds that had built up on either side of us found their path unobstructed once more. I waved to the guard as we passed. He nodded and reached up to adjust the brim of his baseball cap.

"Pull up over there," I said to BB, indicating an empty spot at the far end of the parking lot. Suddenly, a black SUV I hadn't noticed before pulled in front of us, blocking our way. The sound of screeching tires made me turn around. Another SUV had done the same thing behind us, boxing us in.

I reached for the door handle. Before I could get my bearings, men in navy-blue windbreakers emblazoned with what seemed like every letter in the alphabet – DHS, ATF, FBI, NYPD – poured out of every nook and cranny of the park grounds, guns leveled at our heads, screaming for us to put our hands up. My door was wrenched open. Several rough hands grabbed me by my arm and shirt collar and dragged me from the truck. I landed hard on the pavement. A knee was driven into my spine and my arms were twisted behind my back. As the handcuffs bit into my wrists, I tried to turn my head to look for BB, to see if somehow he had managed to get away, but a hand the size of a center fielder's glove palmed the back of my skull and pressed my face into the asphalt. "Stop resisting!" a voice said.

Resisting, I thought? There was no need to resist. My path was charted before pharaohs walked the earth. This was the trial I had expected, the final test of my faith. I had no doubt I would pass. The Gods appoint the end before they appoint the means. I had suffered already; I would suffer more. The stars dwarf our troubles, yet are themselves only the tiniest glimmers in the grand design. As I lay there, contemplating, I felt myself being lifted, borne up and ushered into the back of an unmarked car. We sped from the premises, surrounded by a phalanx of police cars blaring their sirens and flashing their lights. I studied the faces of the people on the street outside who had stopped to gawk, those who could not see me through the impenetrable tint of the car windows, and bade them farewell as I was spirited away.

Chapter 14

My cell is four feet by five feet, too small to do much but sleep or sit on my bed and write. The FBI Agents who visit me from time to time tell me I'm being held in an "Ultramax" prison, one step up from the Federal Supermax in Colorado. I'm the facility's sole prisoner. In fact, I'm one of only a handful of people who knows it exists. "The conditions are terrible," said Agent Stone, the one with the handlebar mustache. "The lawyers say it violates multiple international human rights treaties. But we're pretty sure that in your case no one will mind." He had the look of a child on Christmas morning surveying his presents beneath the tree. "We're really excited to give the place a whirl!"

They had been surveilling me for months. Every movement I made had been closely monitored, my conversations recorded, my face-to-face meetings photographed and catalogued. Undercover agents had infiltrated nearly every facet of my life – they were there on Brathwaite's campus, in my hometown in Pennsylvania, on the bus that had taken me to Lincoln, and inside "my compound in Utah", by which I guess they meant Fear-Gods' palace. Even our broker and the ex-Soviet general who had sold us the bomb had been FBI plants. The "bomb" itself was a fake, nothing more than an old casing stuffed with wires and parts from a decommissioned Xerox machine.

"BB?" I said. "Was he one of you, too?"

"Who?" said Agent Griggs, the one who looked like a weasel. Everyone I spoke with claimed they had never heard of BB.

They tell me I'm being charged with multiple violations under Title 18 of the U.S. Code, Chapter 113B - Terrorism, including Attempted Use of Weapons of Mass Destruction, Attempted Bombing of Places of Public Use, Acts of Nuclear Terrorism, and Attempt to Commit Nuclear Holocaust – 2nd Degree. "Seems like overkill," I said, but the Agents brought me a copy of the relevant statutes and reviewed them with me, and I have to admit they've got a point.

"If I'm such a dangerous criminal," I said, "why do you let me have a pen? Aren't you afraid I'll try to stab you with it and fight my way out?"

"Not really," said Agent Beekman, the one with the greasy hair.

"What if I stab myself?"

"Be my guest. You'd be saving us all a lot of time."

Sentiments like that have left me feeling down lately. To cope, I've taken to meditating for at least thirty minutes every evening. (I assume it's the evening, as it falls within the few hours between when my dinner arrives and I go to bed. There are no windows in my cell, nor am I ever allowed outside for fresh air or exercise. The lights in my cell do not fluctuate but operate at a perpetual half-glow, just the right amount of illumination to make both my waking and sleeping hours uncomfortable. For all I know my meditation sessions could be taking place in the morning, which would mean the guards have been serving me "fiesta pizza" and microwaved Salisbury steak for breakfast all this time. This realization has diminished my appetite significantly.)

I like to sit and stare at a particular spot on the wall of my cell. On first glance, my cell walls seem to possess a perfect uniformity – no cracks or other blemishes, no slanted or uneven blocks. Each block measures exactly two-and-three-quarters finger lengths (my preferred unit of measurement) in height and width, so that the mortar forms a grid pattern, like a net surrounding me. But after weeks and months of studying the walls I managed to locate a tiny chip in the mortar between the fourth and fifth blocks of the third column to the left of my cell door. It was difficult to notice in the gloomy light, but once I found just the right angle the discoloration became apparent and could be spotted easily from a sitting position near the head of my bed.

For hours on end I focus my eyes on this chip, until my mind is cleared of all else. This is what the

Indians call *Dhyana* – sustained attention, the application of one's mind to a chosen point of concentration. I learned this from the *Mahasaccaka Sutta,* the 36th part of the *Majjhima Nikaya*, which rather astonishingly was among the few dozen books stuffed onto the shelves of the prison's library cart. From the *Majjhima Nikaya*, I taught myself to be mindful of my breathing (*anapanasati*), mindful of the impurities of the body (given the quality of food I was being served, it was difficult not to be mindful of them), and to contemplate the Buddha's 32 characteristics (of which I possessed, by my own count, seven).

Time slips further and further away from me. Days blend into weeks, which blend into months; I can no longer distinguish between them. The FBI Agents continue to visit my cell. They ask me open-ended questions, let me prattle on to my heart's content. I can tell they are bored, probably wishing they were anywhere else but sharing my dull, subterranean nightmare, but they never interrupt or try to hurry the proceedings. They are waiting for something useful, a nugget of discernible truth buried in my ramblings. That's the reason they let me have a pen. Every time, right before they're about to wrap up their session with me, one of the Agents asks to "borrow" my notebook for a few minutes, with a promise to return it as soon as they're finished. Making copies, no doubt. Analyzing my writings for clues as to who my associates were, who conspired with me to blow up Manhattan. True to their word, they always bring it back. I wish them the best of luck, and if they discover the Truth in my words, I pray they will share it with me before I am taken to the executioner's block.

My meditation continues unabated. I have traveled deeper into the self than I knew was possible, channeling the mind's eye through that same, minute crack in the mortar. Within minutes of focusing I can make the walls of my cell evaporate, leaving me face to face with my *atman* – my transcendent, innermost essence – in the infinite void. I have achieved *Samadhi*, the eighth limb.

BB visits me from time to time. Never when the guards or the FBI is present; he waits until I'm alone, when we can talk freely. I'll be eating a meal or writing or trying to meditate, and all of a sudden BB is there, perched on the edge of my bed with some urgent message he needs to deliver. "Word from Plymouth," he might say. "Our contacts in Ukraine say they can deliver another bomb. The Seneschal is in hiding, but we're gathering the necessary funds. Stay strong and keep your wits about you. Steps are being taken to secure your release."

"What steps?" I said. "No one knows this place exists. I'm not even sure we're inside the United States."

BB smiled confidently. “Courage, old friend – I’ve had another dream. Your destiny lies outside this place. The universe has preordained it. You *will* escape.”

Enough, I told him. Enough dreams and premonitions and predictions. “If you’re right and I really am chained at the wrist to Fate’s book, then nothing you say or do will change anything,” I said. “Please, just leave me in peace!”

For a time, he respected my wishes, but little by little he began appearing again, always urging me not to give up hope and to “stick to the plan”. Finally, I told the FBI about BB’s clandestine visits. I’d had enough of him, the constant interruptions. I confessed everything – Fear-Gods, the Ukrainians, the new bomb, the escape plans, all of it. Agent Carmichael, the one with the small mole on his right cheek, scoffed. “Insanity defense,” he said to Agent Stone. “I knew that would be his play.”

Stone rolled his eyes. “Nicely predicted, Carnac. I can see why you were 37th in your class.”

On my most recent sojourn inward, my *atman* presented itself to me as a radiant light. It passed through me as if I were made of glass, filling my body and producing within me a sense of overwhelming bliss. Then a figure began to form in the void – little more than an indefinite blob at first, but coalescing into the shape of a beautiful, four-armed woman dressed all in white. In two of her hands, she held a book and a pen. She neither spoke to me nor wrote me a message, yet I felt as though I understood her purpose, as if she were transmitting her thoughts telepathically. With a solemn bow she folded her arms inward and knelt before me, the contours of her body growing hazy once more. Then she began to liquefy and stretch out into a meandering river, its jade waters wending their way past my feet on their journey across the cosmic fabric.

I looked upriver toward the water's source and saw a white object approaching me, bobbing along on the rippling current. When it was near enough, I saw that it was a swan, tall and elegant. As it drew even, it fluttered its wings and exited the water to stand beside me. With a rhythmic whistling it craned its neck to gesture toward the space behind me. I turned around and was confronted by a large hill where the void had just been, stretching hundreds of feet into the air. A loud 'crack' sounded above me. A boulder had broken loose near the top of the hill and was careening down the slope in my direction. My first impulse was to backpedal, but when I turned, I saw that the river had grown wider. Its waters were so swift I would surely drown if I tried to cross it.

I looked up again at the boulder, tumbling end over end and picking up speed as it descended. It seemed to be cutting a path directly toward where I stood, but the hillside's terrain was uneven and dotted with rocky outcrops. I decided to stay calm, observe. My patience seemed to have been rewarded when the boulder started veering steadily to the left, but no sooner had I begun moving to my right than it took a sudden bounce and switched directions, freezing me in my tracks. I decided to wait a little longer, until the boulder had cleared the rocky area at the top of the slope and reached the grassy section below, where its path should become clearer. I held my position, observing, analyzing.

The boulder continued to roll, gathering speed. It had passed the hill's midpoint. For the first time I could see how fast it was moving, no longer rolling but skipping down the slope like a stone across the surface of a lake. Three-quarters of the way down now. My blood froze. There was no longer time for me to get out of the way. Muscles paralyzed, I crumpled to my knees, falling forward until my forehead was pressed against the ground. Above me came the 'thump, thump' of the boulder, like the approaching footsteps of a vengeful deity. Crying out, the swan spread its wings. It lunged into the air, ascending higher and higher above me, far from the sounds of my pathetic prayers.

CPSIA information can be obtained
at www.ICGtesting.com
Printed in the USA
BVHW071611060421
604327BV00003B/219

9 781949 472318